Deep Blue Truth

written by

Ava Armstrong

Chapter 1

Nick Kozlovksy took one last bite of the cheeseburger, stuffed it into the bag, and crumpled it in a moment of exasperation. He'd promised himself to eat better. All that time at the gym wasn't slimming him down. The scale still tipped 215, and even at six feet, his health insurer, the guy in HR—no one—was going to be happy with his progress. By now, the burger had become cold and unappealing. He tossed it into the backseat of the Crown Vic, reminding himself muscle weighed more than fat.

He rolled down the window and the scent of freshly fallen rain rushed in. Motor oil, asphalt, and moist cleansed air mingled to create an aroma only a gearhead could appreciate. The first drops of precipitation had fallen on this dark August evening. Street lamps reflected a blurred sheen off the pavement as he made the third pass through his sector. Even though the night was young, things had been busy in the Bermuda Triangle for the last few days. He'd been dispatched to haul off the usual boosters at the Stop 'N Shop. A couple of young drag racing fools tried out the newly laid pavement and earned themselves reckless driving charges. Down the road, Bubba's strip club had a few bar fights that kept him busy. All routine.

As he waited at the red light, his eyes automatically drifted toward the Cherryfield Methadone Clinic. They stayed open until 9 PM and, if he could, he always hung close. Odds were, he'd be called to remove an unruly addict, or possibly more than one. That completed the Bermuda Triangle. Shit happened in his sector that had no rhyme or reason. Being fresh off his rookie probationary period for three years, Nick was awarded this delightful beat to prove himself ~ at least that's what he surmised.

It was at that moment he saw it, out of his left peripheral -- but couldn't believe his eyes. A blacked-out Mustang blew through the red light at the intersection, and almost clipped his cruiser. Who could be so stupid as to run a red light at an intersection with a clearly marked police cruiser sitting there? His brawny arm turned the steering wheel right as he punched the accelerator. His other hand clicked on the lights and siren. Then he called dispatch.

"Unit 12 in pursuit of black Mustang. Suspicious vehicle driving recklessly, near intersection of Main and Parkway, now heading north on Parkway."

At first it seemed it would be a normal traffic stop. Dispatch acknowledged the call and requested another officer to assist. The black Mustang gave him a run before it pulled to the side at the end of Parkway where it turned into a dark and rural no-man's land. He left the lights on full tilt and cut the siren. As his shoe touched the ground, the door of the vehicle in front of him sprang open and the large occupant emerged. He had to be six-four, lean, wearing a dark jacket. Whoever he was, the stranger bolted into the brush nearby, headed for a heavily wooded area.

"Stop right there!" Nick yelled in his controlled but angry voice. As he gave chase, he cursed himself for losing the driver in the darkness. He peered into the shadows, his eyes followed the beam of his flashlight. He feared the running man might have a weapon. This could be a trap. Nick's heart pounded as he drew his sidearm. His mind raced as he ordered one more time.

"Stop, get down on the ground – now!"

The suspect emerged, then took a turn and stumbled. Nick wondered if anyone else was in the car, and for a split second his head swiveled as he looked back.

Breathing heavily, Nick spoke into his radio.

"Foot pursuit, Unit 12, north end of Parkway."

At that moment the guy pounced, and was upon him. Taken off his feet, Nick lost all stability as he fell onto his back. His mind speculated twenty different outcomes, all of them bad. He should have called for back-up and waited. He felt the stranger's hand reaching for his weapon already drawn, but Nick held onto it with his right hand and experienced excruciating pain as he struggled to keep it. The punch to his face happened in an instant. After the white flashes of light, he felt dizzy, then lost consciousness.

Sirens and lights approached. The guy was off him. Nick heard someone shouting. Doors slammed. It was Ted Steven's voice.

"Officer down!"

Nick opened his eyes and fingered his weapon still clutched in his right hand. As he tried to breathe and swallow, he choked on the blood trickling down his throat. In a spasm of coughing and pain, he was yanked up from the brush by a strong pair of arms.

"Shit. What the hell happened?" Nick murmured as his hand touched his face. When he pulled it away it was covered with blood. The pain was intense.

"Perp is in custody, Nick. Damn, he hit you hard. You're messed up, buddy. Hey, Nick, look at me." Officer Ted Stevens had concern in his voice as his expert eyes focused on Nick's face. "Come on. I'm taking you to the hospital. I think he broke your nose. Girls won't look at you now, with a crooked nose. Come on, baby face!"

Nick let Stevens push him into the front of his cruiser and he laid back in the seat. Stevens ran the lights and siren as he called dispatch.

"Unit 16 checking in. Taking officer from Unit 12 to Cherryfield General Hospital for medical treatment."

Dazed by the punch, Nick's head throbbed, but mostly his nose and eyes hurt like hell. *This reminded him of the time he got sucker-punched by one of his mother's drunken boyfriends. The guy was bigger than him, much bigger. During the fist fight, Nick had tumbled down a staircase and got trapped at the bottom in the stairwell with the guy. Nick was 15 years old at that time and had suffered a concussion and a broken nose. This felt eerily similar.*

Nick rolled down the window of the cruiser and spit out gobs of blood.

"Here." Stevens handed him an empty coffee cup. "Spit in this, damn it. I don't want blood all over my patrol car."

Stevens cruised to the curb in front of the *do not park* sign near the emergency entrance and came around to help Nick out of the car. It didn't seem too busy tonight. A few regulars were hanging in the waiting room, Nick recognized them right away from the clinic. Stevens caught the nurse's attention.

"Hey, this guy's bleeding all over me here. Can you take him off my hands, please? I've gotta cover his sector."

Trish, the nurse who noticed him first, came directly to his side.

"Good Lord, what happened to you, Nick?"

"He got into a scuffle. He's swollen even more now than he was five minutes ago. Looks like a broken nose to me." Stevens was now playing a medical doctor. Nick held the paper coffee cup up to his mouth and spit into it again. Somehow, a bandana had appeared in his hand. Must have belonged to Stevens. He held it to his face in an attempt to stop the blood from gushing from his nose.

"Yes, come along. Nick." Her eyes got big when she looked into his face. Nick complied. He could tell by the way she stared at him, he looked pretty bad.

Like all the officers, Nick was familiar with the personnel in the emergency room. He was usually rounding up homeless people who needed medical care or drug addicts who'd overdosed and he'd drop them off when the wagon couldn't get there quickly enough. Trish was a middle-aged mother of two, sturdy and efficient with red hair pulled into a pony tail. He'd delivered plenty of bashed up victims to Trish in the ER, but she never paid much attention to him, or so it seemed. She ushered him into a tiny room with a curtain and motioned to the doctor walking by. She spoke in hushed tones and he could barely hear her.

"This is important. He's hurt badly."

Trish returned to his side and took off his blood-soaked blue jacket and shirt. Nick had never been a good patient. The few times he'd been in the emergency room; he wasn't exactly compliant. He didn't like to be the center of attention or fawned over for some minor injury. But he liked Trish and didn't intend to give her a hard time.

"Hey, you're looking at my face here, right? Why do I need to take my clothes off?" He could barely get the words out.

Trish's smile disappeared as she looked straight into his now swollen eyes.

"Listen, Nick. You're stripping down and I'm putting a gown on you. Now don't give me a hard time."

He sensed her hands as she removed his pants in one swift motion and she covered the front of him with a soft cotton hospital garment, expertly tying it in the back. Her voice was all business.

"Sit your butt on that bed."

"Damn, I don't want anyone to see me like this."

"Sit on that bed and stop talking. The doctor will be right in."

As Trish spoke the words, a woman walked in and faced him. She was serious, but calm. Her blue eyes met his. No smile. Before she introduced herself, she articulated orders to Trish.

"I need an ice pack right away, and his medical history. I'll get his vitals."

Then the woman turned to Nick and put her hand on his. Her touch was firm but soothing, as if she had done this a thousand times. He had a feeling he was going to do what she wanted, whether he liked it or not.

"I'm Doctor Robertson." She spoke calmly as she slipped the blood pressure cuff onto his arm, then switched it out for a larger one. After she took his blood pressure, her finger located his pulse.

"Can you tell me what happened…Officer Kozlovsky?"

Nick's eyes focused on her face as he rattled off the details of the incident. She looked up occasionally as she efficiently took notes on an iPad. Her eyes were a pale blue, her hair the color of caramel, long and loose. Oh damn. She was beautiful. He'd never seen her before. He was tongue-tied, embarrassed she was seeing him like this, vulnerable, in a damned hospital gown. He finished his little story and wanted to see how far he could get with her.

"That's it. I got punched. So, I can take an ice pack and go?" Nick exhaled.

Her hand moved to his shoulder and he caught a whiff of her scent. She smelled better than the rain, he caught a trace of warmth and honey. He liked the feeling of her hand on his shoulder. But, he pushed against her as he started to rise off the bed.

"Mr. Kozlovsky – please!" Doctor Robertson's hand firmly held him. "You're not leaving this hospital for at least a few hours. According to the report I have here from the officer who found you – you were unconscious. We need to observe you for signs of a concussion and I need to treat your broken nose."

Nick laid back as she adjusted the head of the bed upward. Trish was at the doctor's side with a tray full of items. Doctor Robertson managed a little smile.

"I need to clean you up and I'm going to give you some pain medication. Do you have any allergies?"

"No ma'am." Staring at her took his mind off the pain for a little while. Her fingers were long and elegant, and he noticed the absence of a ring. She wore tiny stud earrings, he caught a glimpse of them when she pushed her hair aside. They looked like a fleur de leis design. He immediately assumed she was religious. Probably upper-class, old money, an over-achiever. She had to be married or have a boyfriend. She was just too damned beautiful to be on her own.

"Just a moment." She acted as if she'd forgotten something. Nick was enjoying the view. She reached into her white jacket pocket and pulled out something, then scooped her hair up with one swift motion. With her hair pulled back, he could scrutinize her features, which were perfect in his estimation. Her complexion was ivory, flawless. Thick brown eyelashes framed her light blue eyes. Her lips were full, soft, with a hint of lipstick. When she smiled there were dimples. *Damn, I'm*

falling in love with a woman I've never met before.
Nick felt his mouth curl into a smile, but even
moving his lips hurt.

It took about thirty minutes for the pain
reliever to kick in. It didn't do much for the pain.

Doctor Robertson proceeded to clean his face
methodically. She was close enough that he could
smell the garlic on her breath. He loved garlic, too.

"What'd you have for dinner?" He gazed
directly into her eyes.

"A meatball. Why do you ask? Are you
hungry?"

"Yeah." He saw a flicker of compassion on
her face.

"I can order you something. Crackers?"

"No, I want a meatball with garlic like you
had." Nick was trying to get a rise out of her and it
was working. She'd either think he was cute or a
pain in the ass. He was hoping for the former.

"Trish, tell Leo to take my car over to
Lentini's for a couple of meatballs." Doctor
Robertson tossed her car keys to Trish, then
washed her hands and continued.

"There, I've got your face cleaned. Now, I need to ask you to not blow your nose for at least eight hours. I want to stop the bleeding. This part might be a bit uncomfortable. Take a deep breath, Nick, let it out and close your eyes."

Nick did as Doctor Robertson asked. Her hand was on the bridge of his broken nose and she pulled it, firmly. Oh man, she pulled it hard and he couldn't breathe at all for a moment. She might as well have kicked him in the nuts. Then, out of nowhere, she started packing gauze into each nostril. He could only imagine how he looked right now.

"After I've finished packing your nostrils with gauze, I'll give you an ice pack. You'll need to breathe through your mouth tonight. Ten minutes with the ice on, then ten minutes with the ice off -- we'll help you with that. I just want to make sure there's no further damage. I'm waiting for the CT results."

"Yeah, and those damned meatballs."

With that, she laughed. And, he was pleased he got to see her dimples again. She had a cute laugh, genuine and feminine. Her eyes sparkled when she looked at him. He could get used to gazing into those eyes.

"You can call me Nick."

"Okay – I'm sorry to say this – but you're going to have two black eyes, Nick."

"Great. I won't need to get a Halloween costume this year.

He made her smile again ~ *good*.

"I won't need to take time off from work for this, will I?"

"Let's take it one day at a time, or one hour at a time."

Nick could tell she was trying to maintain her professional demeanor, but he knew she wanted to laugh. She coiled a piece of gauze around his head. He imagined he looked like a mummy ready for the tomb. His head was throbbing, but when he studied her face, he forgot about it momentarily. He forgot about everything, really. Staring at her as she packed up the tray, he ignored the sounds of the other patients in the cubicles next to them, the doors opening and closing, the voices around them. Everything faded away. It was as if nothing else in the world mattered at that moment except her. And he had no idea who she was or where she came from, but he wanted to know everything about her.

"What's your name?" He wanted to know her first name. And what he didn't find out now, he'd get later from the other employees in the ER.

"You can call me Doctor Robertson."

He noticed the slight blush. "I meant your *first* name."

There was hesitation before her eyes met his. "Grace, if you must know."

"Grace. I like that name. Bet you were called Gracie as a little girl."

"Actually, yes." The hint of a smile appeared.

"You're new here."

"Not so new. I moved to Cherryfield about eight months ago."

"No ring. You're not married."

She didn't answer right away, *not a good sign*.

She changed the subject. "You're distracting, Nick. I'll be right back."

She hadn't answered his question. Nick had the feeling she'd just shot him down, in a nice way. All the romantic stuff he'd been daydreaming about for the past hour was probably for naught. A chick like her would never look at a grunt like him. She was a doctor; he was a lowly patrolman. He looked at himself in the mirror on the tabletop before him. At least he didn't lose any teeth. It could've been worse.

As Grace pushed the curtain aside, he looked up. Her dimples dazzled him and his pulse raced.

"Your meatballs are here."

Her pale blue eyes were softer and there was tenderness in her voice. Just before she turned away, her gaze lingered with his and he caught a glimpse of the deep blue truth that resided within. He had stirred something inside. He just hoped the first impression was a good one.

When he took the warm cardboard container with the aroma of garlic from her, his hand brushed hers. He intentionally grasped her slender hand with his big one.

"Thank you, ma'am."

She withdrew slowly and turned away.

"You're welcome, officer. I know your job's not an easy one. I appreciate all that you do."

He watched as she moved into the hallway and on to the next patient without looking back, the model of efficiency. But he imagined she didn't do this for every patient. She'd made him feel appreciated, something that always caught him by surprise.

Eating was painful and awkward. He had to breathe between bites and the ever-present taste of his own blood made everything taste funny. Nevertheless, the meatballs were gone within minutes and the gnawing hunger in his stomach stopped long enough for him to close his eyes. After a long draw of ice cold water, he allowed his head to sink into the pillow. Sleep overcame him immediately. At one point, he felt a hand on his face holding an ice pack. His eyes were closed but he knew it was her. He remained still as her long fingers swept through his disheveled hair. How did she know he loved that? If this was a dream, he didn't want to awaken.

Chapter 2

Grace Robertson was near the end of her shift in the ER with a half-smile on her lips. Nick Kozlovsky was a pleasant distraction. She had met most of the police officers, but hadn't met him face-to-face until tonight. For the past eight months, when he dropped off someone for treatment, she noticed he exited quickly. Grace had craned her neck more than once to catch a glimpse of him. That baby face was the first thing she noticed. He was young, new to the force, and she read him as a bit shy. That was before tonight. She couldn't have been more mistaken.

"Are we moving him to a room?" Trish was at her side.

"Yes. I want to keep him overnight for observation."

"Might be better if *you* tell him. He's obstinate."

"Yeah. I hadn't noticed." Grace moved in the direction of Nick's cubicle.

When she entered, he was sound asleep with the meatball container on his chest. His ice pack had been refilled, but he didn't have it on his face.

She placed her hand on his right arm and noticed a large bruise. His eyes fluttered and connected with hers immediately.

"He tried to take my gun. That left a mark, huh?"

"Yes. Quite a bruise here." Her fingers skimmed the well-formed bicep and she found herself wanting to explore further. "Are there any other injuries I don't know about?"

"Yes. You can check every inch of me, if you'd like. I'll roll over if you want. Moving is slightly painful."

Wondering if he was serious or just joking with her, Grace loosened the ties of the gown and ran her hands over his chest. She had never examined a guy who worked out this much. His pectoral muscles were firm and his abdominal core was solid. Her eyes were fixed to the tattoo of an eagle on his chest. She suddenly realized she was performing the examination more for her own curiosity than medical reasons. Nick's eyes were closed and he made no sound. Her hands moved lower toward his hips and he turned his head and she caught his grin.

"Yes. Lower." He whispered.

Grace pulled the blanket over him and stepped back.

"Very funny, Kozlovsky. You're staying overnight for observation."

"What?" He sat up and she saw him wince. "No, I've got to go to work tonight. I'll sleep this off in my apartment. *Really*. I promise, doc. I'll take the ice pack with me."

"If I discharge you, I'm responsible if something happens. You know that." Grace parsed her words carefully. It was difficult for her to maintain her professional demeanor with this comedian.

"Really. I promise. I'll go home and rest." His blue eyes implored her. She felt as if she was arguing with a 215-pound four-year old.

"All right. I want you to check in with your primary care doctor. I'm writing the name of a cosmetic surgeon for you. You're going to need to have that nose redone. It's called a deviated septum."

"Yes, ma'am. Deviant."

She had all she could do not to laugh. She handed him a note scribbled on her business card, then watched as he slid out of bed. His hospital gown opened in the back as he picked up his pants from the chair. She had the distinct feeling he wanted her to watch. Even though she didn't want to, she couldn't stop herself from staring. His backside was as well-developed as his front and there was ink on his back, too. He glanced over his shoulder, caught her gaze, and she turned away blushing. *Argh.* She knew she shouldn't have looked. As she moved out of the room, she heard Nick's voice.

"Hey, thanks, Grace."

She didn't turn around. It was too tempting.

"You're welcome, Officer Kozlovsky."

"You can call me Nick."

It was well past midnight and she'd been on her shift since 3 PM. Grace yawned and stretched, then closed out the medical file of Nick Kozlovsky on her iPad. He was the perfect specimen of health. No illnesses, no sexually transmitted diseases, good blood work. He only visited the ER for occasional injuries. Grace Robertson waved hello to the new nurses coming in and briefed the doctor replacing her.

The fresh night air felt refreshing on her face as she strode toward her Land Rover parked in the reserved spot. The parking lot security lights highlighted the white gauze around his head and he made her jump a little. As she approached her vehicle, Nick Kozlovsky was standing next to it.

"How the heck did you get here so quickly?"

"I'm fast."

"Not fast enough to stop that guy from punching your face in."

"I need a lift home. I live a few blocks away. I just don't want to walk home looking like a zombie. I need to get my uniform cleaned."

Grace's eyes traveled over him. The dried blood on his uniform did look awful. And, his head wrapped in gauze and eyes almost swollen shut gave him a pitiful appearance.

"Okay. Get in." She unlocked the door and he slid into the seat.

She felt his eyes on her as she started the engine and swiveled her head to back out of the parking space.

"If you backed in, you'd not have to pull out like this."

"Thanks. I'll remember that."

"It's just that I always park like that with the cruiser. Never know when I'm going to jump in and take off."

"That makes sense." She glanced his way a few times and noticed how he filled up the seat of her Land Rover. This guy was big, a knuckle-dragger. Thick neck, long arms, wall-to-wall muscles. She imagined he lived at the gym and had all sorts of women hanging around him.

For the rest of the brief ride he was quiet except for giving directions to his apartment, which happened to be in a seedy section of Cherryfield. She pulled up to the curb of the four-plex turn-of-the-century building with peeling green paint. Nick grabbed his gear and hopped out.

"Thanks, Grace. I'll see you soon."

"Yeah. I hope not. The ER isn't the sort of place you want to hang out."

She felt herself smiling like an idiot. She noticed the bounce in Nick's step as he bounded up the porch stairs to the back left unit. He'd just had the shit kicked out of him but he still had that spring in his step. He turned for a moment and glanced at her. He nodded in a grateful sort of way. Ah, he was cute, dimples and all. While she drove home, she couldn't get the image of Nick Kozlovsky out of her mind.

What was she thinking? She was a physician now, not in med school. *She had to be careful about getting too attached to coworkers, patients. The situation with Michael should've taught her that lesson. It was love at first sight and lasted for four years. Michael was her professor in medical school, had exciting friends, and oh yeah, he was hot. Very hot. She sat in the front row in every class she had with him. It was full-on every time for the first two years. He'd made love to her in his office and every hidden spot on campus. But little by little, over time, Grace realized Michael was getting all the benefits in the relationship and after the hot sex, she spent much of her time alone. If she brought up the fact that he was married, Michael would dismiss the conversation and cleverly change the subject. Once he told Grace she was bordering on hysteria when she suggested he divorce his wife. That night she cried herself to sleep after he left the tiny apartment she had taken across the street from the school. Convenient for him, that was.*

Her first year as a doctor in the ER at Cherryfield had been hard enough. The schedule was grueling, the work difficult and sometimes heartbreaking. But, living alone made it easier to focus on her profession. There were no distractions. She didn't even have a pet. Being a doctor had consumed her life, but that helped alleviate the emotional pain. She wondered if it was healthy to exchange one addiction for another. *Probably not.*

Although she was hungry, she tossed her clothing on the floor and started the shower. She always washed immediately after work. While lathering her hair, she viewed the late August moon through the open bathroom window and felt a pang of regret for summer's leaving. Autumn always made her think of Michael. And, right now he was the *last* person she wanted haunting her thoughts. She'd blocked him from her mind and all her social media accounts. She even blocked his number on her phone. But, she couldn't just wash the thought of him away with the grime of her workday. He had inhabited her thoughts for the last four years of her life.

As she toweled dry she looked at herself in the full-length mirror. She was thirty years old and had accomplished every goal she'd set forth, except for one. Even though she had friends and family available at a moment's notice, she felt incredibly empty inside. Her girlfriends were all married or engaged. She was the only holdout in the group.

She turned away from the mirror, hung her towel and wrapped herself in a warm flannel robe. After wolfing down a bowl of cereal, and brushing her teeth, Grace slid between the soft cotton sheets. It was important that she fall asleep with a positive thought instead of a negative one -- at least that's what her therapist told her.

What positive thought could she conjure? She was looking forward to the coming Labor Day weekend, which she had off. She hadn't had any time off except her scheduled days since she started at the ER. She couldn't wait to crack a beer and laugh with good friends. That was a pleasant thought to lull her to sleep.

But another person occupied her mind before she fell asleep in her small bungalow in the east end of Cherryfield – Nick Kozlovsky. His thick dirty-blond hair and stunning blue eyes stayed with her. She couldn't stop herself from running her fingers through his thick blonde hair as she held the ice pack on his face. It wasn't that he was gorgeous and she liked looking at him, although she had to admit he was visually appealing. There was something about him ~ warmth, sincerity. Those deep blue eyes told her Nick Kozlovsky was different. Tough on the outside, but tender on the inside. He was a man who knew who he was. And that's what she wanted to explore. She wanted to get inside of him, feel his arms around her, his breath on her neck. His eyes were gentle, understanding, yet a lethal calmness resided there. Everything about Nick made her feel, feminine, and oh, so unprofessional.

Chapter 3

Nick woke in the morning to a throbbing headache and took an over-the-counter pain reliever, then drank a glass of fresh orange juice, one of the few things in his refrigerator. He filled a half gallon jug with cold water and packed his gear for the gym. He climbed into the 1987 Jeep Renegade with more miles on it than he wanted to admit. He'd kept the thing running with sheer ingenuity and luck. His buddy, Shane, owned a junkyard and had three or four Renegades from the 80's. He gave Nick a bargain when he came to pillage parts.

"Damn. When're you gonna pop for a new set of wheels?" Shane asked him last week.

"Not in the near future. I don't make that kind of money."

"Shit. You're a cop now. You've passed the junior cop stage."

"Nah. My money goes to rent and stuff like that. No leftovers for fun things." Nick smiled. "But, hell. I'm doing something I love. So, that's some sort of pay right there, isn't it?"

Like everything else in his life, he'd deal with that when the time came. What Shane didn't know was that Nick was helping to support his sisters living with his aunt. Sure, he skimped on things for himself, but then that wasn't so alien to him. Putting himself first wasn't something he could even imagine. He liked older vehicles anyway. Plus, he was happy with the Renegade. He got a discount on a black paint job and customized it, badass style. Lots of people asked about it when he pulled into a parking lot.

At the drive-through, the girl at the window winked at him when he picked up his order for a double fried egg on a bagel with cheese. He ate it while driving. Couldn't run on no fuel. He was ravenous today.

A motorcycle buzzed by and he watched it zoom ahead. It reminded him of the Harley he had purchased in the spring. It was a huge splurge for him, a used Harley super-low. He felt on top of the world when he revved that engine and headed out to the countryside. Sometimes he'd ride for hours alone. Other days, one of the many charities he was affiliated with would organize a run. Soon, he'd be putting it into storage for the winter, sad thought that was.

At the red light, he noticed a man climbing out of a ravine near Bud's gas station. Next door was Bud's diner, which was in his sector. He'd eaten more meals there than he could count. The man looked at him, then quickly turned away, as if he had something to hide. Curious, Nick pulled into the station to fuel up. He walked to the edge of the deep gulley and noticed a makeshift tent down there and some other items. One of the many homeless people in the area, no doubt. Nick moved to his vehicle as he heard the pump click off.

"Hey, can you spare some change?"

Nick heard the raspy voice and spun around. The guy was scruffy, fairly young, and smelled pretty bad, even from a distance.

"You living down there, man?"

"Yeah. Been here all summer. You look familiar."

Nick noticed a dog sitting perfectly still next to the man. The canine looked like a stray ~ no collar, underfed. The dog and the man had similar characteristics in that respect.

"What're you doing living down here, may I ask?" Nick was curious.

"I've been here since I got back from Afghanistan." His eyes looked away as he said the words.

"You're a veteran?"

"Yeah. Hey, I know your face from somewhere…" the stranger hesitated. "You're that cop. The one that drives through here all the time at night. You probably don't remember, but you saw me in the parking lot behind the diner once."

Nick remembered. This was the guy dumpster diving for garbage after hours. He'd thought he was just another addict living on the streets. No harm, no foul. He'd moved him on his way and now recalled the conversation. The guy told him he was living nearby. Nick just didn't realize he meant a tent in the gutter.

"What's your name, soldier?"

"Paco. And, this is my best bud, Diesel. I found him wandering around. I called the shelter but they said no one was looking for a dog that fit his description, so I just kept him. He's good company. Smart. He protects me at night when I'm sleeping. Sort of like having an alarm system with me all the time, you know?"

Nick moved to put the fuel handle back in its place on the pump. Then he turned to Paco.

"You said you need money. Are you using drugs? Be honest with me."

"I smoke pot once in a while when I can get it. It's for the pain. And, I get methadone at the clinic. Can't live without that, man. If you're curious about what I need money for – it's to get medical care for Diesel and dog food. Plus, I need money for bus fare to get to the homeless shelter for my meals."

"Why don't you stay at the shelter? They've got beds…"

"Nah. Come on man. First of all, they won't let me keep Diesel with me. They've got bed bugs, too. And lice. And, some diseases I don't really want to get. I've slept in barracks for a good part of my life. I'm sick of that shit. I'm a free man now. I can do as I please, as long as I'm not breaking the law. Right?"

"Yes. You're right." Nick handed Paco a twenty-dollar bill.

"Hey, I'm going to the gym. Want to tag along and get a shower? I can bring a guest free of charge."

"What about Diesel?"

"We'll feed him and let him take a nap in the owner's office. I know him well."

"No. I've got to get Diesel to the veterinary clinic. But, thank you – I didn't catch your name."

"Nick. I'll be out here on the night shift. You'll see me. Hey, don't be a stranger."

As Nick opened the door to his Jeep, Paco said something that stopped him.

"That guy beat you pretty bad last night. He's a runner. He was high on a synthetic drug that he pushes a lot around here. Bad stuff, that Molly shit. Really bad. He made a few deals right here in your territory."

"And, you witnessed him attacking me last night? Would you be willing to make a statement? Because this low-life has a good attorney. The dash-cam on my car didn't catch it. We were off to the side, out of view." Nick waited for a moment as Paco shifted nervously.

"Yeah, I'll make a statement – to you. And, *only* you. I don't want to get involved. I want to remain anonymous."

"Okay. I'll take your statement right here; you sign it on the hood of my Jeep. Nick found a legal pad and a pen and helped Paco with his eye witness account. After it was signed, Nick put it into his backpack.

"I have one other favor to ask." Nick held his breath before continuing. "If you see shit like this, would you be willing to do some investigative work for me, on the down-low? I'd pay you cash. No one would know except you and me."

Paco's eyes roamed around as the town began to come to life. Traffic had picked up. Nick got the distinct feeling Paco didn't like standing in a gas station parking lot in broad daylight with him.

"Let me think about it. I'll see you tonight." Paco moved away, and Diesel followed.

Nick got into his Jeep and began to roll away from the gas station. In his rearview mirror, the silhouette of Paco and Diesel in the early morning light made him shiver. Damn, as soon as late September came, it would be getting really cold outside. There was no way Paco could continue living in the ravine in a tent. He hoped the guy was being honest with him and not scurrying around the corner to buy some crack or heroin.

As he carried his bag through the gym door, he was greeted with all sorts of comments.

"What the hell happened to you?"

"I hope the other guy looks worse than you do!"

"How many of them worked you over?"

Nick gave them his middle finger. "Yeah, yeah. Wait until it's *your* turn."

"Why didn't you shoot the son-of-a-bitch?" Officer Johnson shouted across the room.

"He was unarmed. Don't want to lose my shield."

Nick didn't exactly want to discuss this in the middle of the gym in front of everyone. He walked into the locker room and stashed his gear. It was time to get on the treadmill and run, then hit the weights for a grueling two-hour workout.

Although some of the guys at the gym could be meatheads, he looked forward to the upcoming Labor Day weekend with his favorites. He'd always wanted to go white water rafting and his best friend, Paul, was getting married. This was Paul's choice for a bachelor party and it was the perfect way to spend the last weekend of summer.

As he finished on the treadmill he wiped the sweat from his face with a towel. The throbbing in his nose was annoying him. He soaked the towel with cold water and held it on his nose for a few minutes. When he took it off he saw Paul walk by.

"Hey, what's the weather forecast?" Nick hadn't paid attention to the radio this morning. He was still daydreaming about the incident, the emergency room, and meeting Grace.

"Rain mostly this week. But Labor Day weekend is supposed to be sunny and warm. Hey, are you all right? I mean, to go white water rafting? You look like you're in a lot of pain, Nick."

"Just bruising, that's all." Nick waved him off. The others in the gym stared at him for the rest of his workout. He hoped in a week the purple and blue marks would be faded and the swelling gone. He'd bring an ice pack with him in the cruiser tonight. He really needed to get the healing process underway.

* * *

Paco moved quickly to the Stop 'N Shop with Diesel by his side. The dog was in sync with him and the smallest gesture or voice command was obeyed without fail.

"Stay here, boy." Paco gestured to the canine and he sat still.

Inside, people stared as Paco slipped into the rest room. He pulled a washcloth out of his backpack and stripped down to his boxer shorts. Within five minutes he'd used the soapy washcloth to wash his entire body and filled the sink with water to rinse off. Lastly, he washed his thick black hair and put the baseball cap back on. He pulled freshly laundered pants and a shirt out of his backpack. Several shoppers came in to use the rest room, and pretended he wasn't there.

He kept a close eye on Diesel as he waited in line at the service desk. The dog stayed put and

Paco smiled as he watched him through the plate glass window. When he got to the clerk he asked for change for the $20 and a Powerball ticket. The guy behind the counter looked him over and handed him the change and the ticket. Paco couldn't wait to step back outside. The stares and whispers made him uncomfortable. Diesel's tail wagged the moment he saw him but he stayed glued to the spot until Paco ruffled his fur.

"Good boy." Paco murmured.

As Paco tapped the side of his leg, Diesel fell into step beside him. The dog was so well trained he'd respond to hand gestures only. Paco spoke lovingly to him because he knew it served to strengthen the bond between them. The walk to the homeless shelter was seven miles. He'd walked much longer distances than that as a soldier. But now the pain in his back was unbearable. Herniated discs, six of them to be exact. And, the last time he'd seen the doctor, he was told there wasn't exactly a surgical fix. But they gave him pain medication. He remembered the first time he took the oxy. *It was great – like magic, no pain.* But in a short period of time, he needed more. When he couldn't get enough, he'd get restless, agitated, and his PTSD got worse. Over time, living outside, he noticed he was getting pain in his legs and arms. He blamed it on exposure to the elements. Lately, his entire digestive process had slowed to the point of stopping on some days. He rarely ate enough food and had lost 30 pounds since returning home.

"Let's take the bus." He whispered to Diesel.

The small group at the bus stop moved away as Paco arrived with his canine. He hoped the driver would be Bill. He was the only one who'd been kind to him about having a service dog ride along. Paco smiled when the bus pulled up and he saw Bill's profile in the driver's window.

"Hey, Paco. How're you today?" Bill smiled.

"Good, sir. And, you?"

"I see you have your faithful service dog with you." Bill said it loudly so that everyone on the bus would understand. It was sort of a routine they had, for which Paco was deeply grateful. Paco took the seat nearest the door and Diesel tucked his canine body close to him.

The bus wound its way through Cherryfield to the nearby city of Wellington, and eventually stopped about a block from the shelter. Paco said his goodbye to Bill and the bus driver winked at him.

A few strangers eyed him as he took his place in the line at the shelter for lunch. The homeless population in Connecticut wasn't a fixed group. They shifted and changed every month or so. More veterans this time. Some of the guys wore a piece of camo or had that hardened look of service. Several men nodded at him in recognition. Not many in the line had bathed in days, maybe weeks. Their thrift-shop clothing was ill-fitting and mismatched. Paco blended right in. As he got to the area where the meals were handed out, he had to have Diesel sit by the exit. This was always the worst moment for him. Paco protected Diesel as much as Diesel protected him. They were both outcasts who looked out for one another. No greater love.

Diesel knew the routine and waited patiently, watching Paco take the tray filled with hot food. Paco stepped away from the other people without eye contact and sat on the ground near the back exit. Half inside the building, half outside. The heat from the kitchen warmed him. Even though it was late August, the nights had started getting cooler, sometimes in the 40's and 50's, enough to make him wish for a warm wool blanket. But, he worried more about Diesel than he did himself. The dog needed a veterinary check-up and it was Paco's goal to find care for the animal. He ate quickly, then let Diesel have the leftovers.

"Hey, Paco. Haven't seen you for a while." Her voice was soft and quiet. She spoke to him as if he was the only person in the room, although the place was filled with more than a hundred people.

"Good. I'm good. Diesel here needs some help. I think he's got worms."

She tapped her iPhone and crouched next to him.

"Got your phone on you?"

Paco's heart swelled with happiness as she read off the number of a veterinarian who'd treat Diesel for free. She said she'd put in a good word for him. Trouble was, this guy was a bus ride away in another town. Getting Diesel there and back would be a challenge. But he didn't want to put his troubles on anyone else. He had skills. He'd find a way.

Paco moved away from her and nodded in appreciation. He remembered the night he was in the ER. She was a doctor – a newly minted one. She hadn't become cynical and stuck-up yet. She probably would, just like the rest of them, eventually. He felt her pale blue eyes on him as he stood and put the empty cardboard tray into the trash can. Then she handed him a folded wool blanket.

"Don't be a stranger." She nodded.

"Thanks, doc." Paco took the blanket from her hands.

Diesel moved toward her and wagged his tail. Paco whistled and the canine instantly moved back in the direction of his master.

"Come on, boy. Time to go home. I'll get you some food tonight."

The bus ride home was filled with working class folks on the low end of the pay scale. Some stared and others smiled, probably realizing there was someone worse off than they were. Yes, they felt lucky, the ones that smiled. Paco always made eye contact with them but never for long. It was his way of saying hello. After shopping at the pet store for dog food and organic worm medicine consisting of garlic and pumpkin seeds, Paco settled in for the night in the ravine. The girl behind the counter had given him a discount and he was thankful. At least it had stopped raining and his small campsite started to dry. As he built a fire, he thought about Nick's offer to be his confidential informant. He already knew all the players in the drug game. All he'd have to do is tap his phone and text a few things and stay out of sight. The money would sure come in handy.

It was time for his nightly trek to the methadone clinic. He always liked to go just before closing time. It wasn't as busy then and Tammy worked the night shift. She was nice to him. Seldom people were. Most turned away or sneered at him openly. Once he got pummeled by a group of teens who roamed the streets looking for trouble. That was a low point. Tammy's soft brown eyes landed on him as he walked through the reception room door. She handed out the methadone while behind a bulletproof window, and smiled.

"Good evening, Paco."

"Hey, Tammy. Have a good night."

He drank the concoction handed to him in a paper cup. Tammy always made him smile. He allowed himself to bask for a moment in her sweetness. Then turned and walked through the exit into the vestibule that led to the cool night air.

Paco and Diesel snuggled up in the tent that night. The rain began later, a light drizzle, and the fire went out. Twice Paco woke to the sound of police sirens. He pulled the woolen blanket tighter around him. Diesel was snuggled up against his back. Eventually, sleep came to him. He dreamt he was back in the barracks at the base in Afghanistan. The rest of the night was filled with faraway voices giving orders, packing his gear, heading out for a mission into the black desert night. A few times he heard the crack of gunfire. His friend lay beside him, killed instantaneously. Paco woke yelling, moving to help his brother, then realized he was sweating and shaking again. Diesel was licking his face, whimpering. When he stood outside, the rain pelted his upturned face like tiny needles. He closed his eyes and welcomed the feeling. It was much better than what he'd just imagined.

Chapter 4

Nick's time was spent detailing his patrol car after the gym. While he scrubbed and vacuumed, the face of Grace Robertson was in the back of his mind. She was one of those chicks who was gorgeous but seemed oblivious, almost uncomfortable, with her beauty. She was all buttoned up, proper-like. Most of the women he'd met who were pretty seemed to be well aware of it. So much so, they used it as leverage in many situations to gain promotions, friendships, and because of their beauty moved to the top of the social strata. But there was a humble quality about Grace. He noticed it when her lashes swept downward and she stifled a smile.

He spent some time digging up all the information he could on Grace Robertson. Before going onto his shift, he propped up his laptop and googled her name. Her life was there before him on her Facebook page. Lots of photographs of sorority sisters and sweeping well-manicured lawns with gardens in upstate New York. There were some funny childhood photos her sister sent to her. A snapshot of her current bungalow was higher up on the timeline. She had many friends, mostly female, but there were a few guys on there, too. The one that he examined closely was Doctor Michael Dean. He looked older than Grace, and had a nervous look about him. Being a doctor, Nick assumed he might've been a classmate. But, once he clicked on Doctor Dean's page, he realized he was a professor at Grace's college and was married. One more thing he noticed. Doctor Dean no longer made comments during the last few months on Grace's Facebook page. Dean's commentary was constant until a certain date, then it stopped. His first thought was Dean could've been a former lover. But he didn't like it when people assumed things about him, so he decided he wouldn't do that with Grace. If he wanted to know something, he'd ask her, in the proper way.

He closed the computer and prepared for his upcoming shift. His cell phone vibrated and he looked down at the text message. Oh damn, it was Kristie and she was pissed. He was supposed to see her today, but had totally forgotten. Her car had something wrong with it again. Her text even looked angry with imbedded ugly red faces in it. He sent a reply. *Sorry, how about tonight? Late.* No answer. Probably more drama than he wanted to deal with anyway.

Before leaving his apartment, he stashed everything in his backpack. He almost forgot the ice pack, and filled it and slid it in the side pocket. He glanced at his reflection in the mirror that hung near the front door. He looked horrible and wondered if they'd even let him work tonight. He mounted the Harley and it roared to life as he sat there in neutral. The familiar *blub blub* always filled him with a sense of exhilaration. The super-low was a used bike. He'd picked it up from a friend who was getting a divorce and the price was right. It was blue, his favorite color. The same blue as Grace's eyes.

At the station, he got his freshly cleaned uniform out of his locker. He had extra money taken out of his meager paycheck to have his uniforms picked up and cleaned, but it was worth every penny. He didn't have a washer and dryer. Plus, the dry cleaner paid attention to details which enhanced his appearance at roll-call. He put a quick shine on his shoes, slicked his hair back and made sure he was at roll-call a few minutes early.

As the other officers filtered in, some comments came his way.

"What happened to you?"

"Did a truck run over you?"

The other officers softly punched his arm on the way by, some smiling and Nick suspected they knew every detail of the incident.

Lieutenant Lee brushed by.

"Good evening, Kozlovsky. Step into my office after roll-call, just for a minute."

"Yes, sir."

At roll call, the usual list of wants were described, drug dealers, prostitutes, BOLO's, and he knew the information would magically appear on his cruiser's iPad screen. Once dismissed, Nick moved toward the doorway to talk with the lieutenant. The stout bald man stood next to his desk, all business, his face filled with concern.

"I didn't want to say anything in front of the other guys, Nick, but are you feeling okay to work tonight? I heard what happened. You should've at least used the taser on that son-of-a-bitch. Don't hesitate if this happens again. You understand?"

"Yes, sir." Nick looked into his superior officer's deep set brown eyes. "I'll be more proactive, sir."

"The bastard who punched your lights out was high on a drug that causes hallucinations. He could've killed you, Nick. I love your heart of gold, but lose it. You've got a shield of gold now, brother. Stay safe. Get the hell out of here." Lieutenant Lee put his hand on Nick's shoulder and shoved him off, his version of a love tap.

Rain and wind cooled Nick's face as he pulled his navy-blue jacket around him. He thought of Paco in the pup tent as he dashed to his cruiser. He checked the lights, siren, radio, and secured his shotgun before taking off. Within seconds, the first call came over the radio. Officer Stevens had stopped a suspected drug dealer on the edge of the Bermuda Triangle, and needed back-up. Nick responded.

"Unit 12 on the way to assist Unit 19."

Nick rolled up on the scene within minutes. Stevens had the guy out of the car on the ground, face planted into the pavement in handcuffs. Nick parked his cruiser and killed the siren.

"I need to search his vehicle." Stevens moved toward the suspect's car.

"I got him." Nick replied as he pulled the suspect to his feet in one swift move. He leaned the dude against the cruiser. After going through the young man's pockets, he noticed he was tensing his gluteal muscles.

"What's the problem here?" Nick growled as he pushed his fingers into the man's butt crack.

"Hey, screw you, pig!"

"Let's drop these pants." Nick ignored the suspect as he yelled obscenities at him.

As Nick glanced at the details on his license, he realized this was no man, he was still a boy of nineteen.

Nick whispered in his ear, "They're using you, man. Don't you *see* that?"

Stevens was next to him. "I searched his car. Look what I found."

Nick glanced at the stacks of money Stevens had in his hands.

"Did you find anything on him?" Stevens asked.

"Yeah, it's up his ass."

"What the --?" Stevens had a quizzical look on his face.

"Yeah, hold him. I'll get it." Nick snapped on a pair of latex gloves and separated the man's legs. Within a moment, he'd fished out a full baggie of oxy from his rear.

This was Steven's collar. The evidence was tagged and bagged in his cruiser and the suspect whisked away to the county jail. Nick never felt good after making a guy like that. If anything, it just gave him feel an empty feeling inside. Shit, the guy was still a teenager. Nick tossed the latex gloves into his trash bag in the back of his cruiser and washed with his ever-present anti-bacterial wipes.

What was he doing at nineteen? He'd just started at Cherryfield Community College, on a grant for underprivileged youth. Being an Eagle Boy Scout had saved his ass. He'd agreed to become a member of the college student patrol, which was no easy feat. Shining a bright flashlight on fellow students doing illegal things didn't exactly make him popular, but it helped him pay his way through college. The rest came out of his pocket. He was a pizza delivery guy when he wasn't patrolling the campus, studying criminal justice, hitting the gym, or smooching a hot chick begging him to do her. Yeah, that was him at nineteen. Not running illegal drugs for dealers and junkies. The Boy Scouts, the Student Patrol ~ that was when he learned what it felt like to be part of something greater than himself. He knew he wanted to be a law enforcement officer. He wanted to make a positive impact on the world. There was no question.

Seconds later, he was dispatched to a domestic situation at Bubba's Strip Club. A report of child abuse was made by a citizen.

"Unit 12 responding to Bubba's."

Bubba's was a place filled with liquor, dancing girls hard up for money, and drugs – lots of drugs. Every night there'd be five or six calls just for Bubba's alone. As he cruised into the parking lot, a female flagged him down. She was tall, blonde, and transgender, no question about that. Nick allowed himself a moment to assess the scene before jumping out of the cruiser. More than one cop had been cornered in that parking lot and beaten hard. He turned off the lights but left his emergency flashers on. The blonde appeared to be alone and had a drink in her hand.

"Pssst, here, over here. There's a kid sleeping in the backseat of this car. I don't know who the parents are. But isn't this child endangerment or something like that?"

Nick stepped out of the cruiser and flashed his light into the blonde's face.

"Can I get your name, please, ma'am?"

"Hell, no. I don't want any part of this. I'm just doing a good deed, that's all." She moved toward the entrance to Bubba's and disappeared. Well, at least she made the call. That's more than most people would do.

Nick clicked his flashlight and looked into the backseat of the sedan. There was a child curled up sound asleep in the back. His automatic license plate recognition told him the car was registered to a Deidre Evans. He knew what he had to do, but would take little pleasure in completing the task. He used his lockout tool and opened the door softly. The interior car light came on and Nick could see the dark-haired boy was maybe six. Nick squatted down and smiled at him.

"Hey, what's your name?" He tried to appear as non-threatening as possible, although he imagined his bruised face probably looked pretty scary to the little guy.

The boy's eyes widened and he scrambled across the seat of the car as far away from Nick as he could get, as he screamed, "No!"

Nick extended his hand in friendship.

"Come on. I'm not going to hurt you. How long have you been sleeping here?"

With some coaxing, the boy got out of the car. Nick radioed for CPS to come to the parking lot. While waiting, he showed the boy his cruiser. Finally, the child gave his name and his mother's name. Henry Evans yawned while Nick explained he'd be having a sleepover tonight.

"What do ya mean? I don't want no sleepover."

"Don't worry. You'll get food and a bed to sleep in and a nice lady will talk with you. It's like an interview. She'll ask you some questions. That's all."

"What about my mom?"

That's the question that always stopped Nick.

"Well, I've got to have a long talk with your mom. That's all. Just a talk, about grown-up stuff."

As he looked into Henry's innocent worried eyes, he realized that was him when he was six years old. He'd slept in hallways while his mother drank her life away with low-life bums. He felt as if he had to protect her from the guys who used her. By the time he was 15, he realized he couldn't protect his mother from herself. He never knew what it was like to sleep in a comfortable bed. He had several younger siblings who peed on him. The mattress never had sheets, just ratty old blankets from the thrift store. In all, he moved 18 times. He knew kids in military families who didn't move that often. It was when the rent money had been used for alcohol, the food stamps sold for cash. His mother would say she was down on her luck. He remembered tossing everything he owned into a green trash bag in the middle of the night and taking a cab to sleep in the home of some distant relative. His mother would send him into the street until he could find a "for rent" sign in a window and a slum lord willing to take on a woman with five children. It was always a place with bed bugs and rats living in the walls. Shangri-La.

Child Protective Services arrived and little Henry was taken away. As he cried for his mother, Nick swallowed hard. Inside Bubba's he found Deidre Evans at the bar drinking shots with her friends. No way did he want her son to witness this. No child should see their mother in this condition. As several people pointed her out, Nick approached Deidre Evans from the side. The bleached blonde hair and smudged make-up looked all too familiar. Her heavy floral perfume mixed with the scent of alcohol nearly made him barf. She was astonished as he took her by the arm and commanded her to stand. Calmly, he placed the handcuffs on her before she could really get into the fight. Her friends called him names and shouted obscenities at him. Nothing he hadn't heard before.

"You're under arrest, Deidre Evans, for child endangerment. You can come along quietly, or make a big dramatic scene. It's no difference to me. You have the right to remain silent…"

She was beyond drunk. She was so intoxicated her pupils couldn't even focus. He wondered if there was more than alcohol in her system. She stumbled without him supporting her. A hoarse voice sounding much older came from her thin red lips.

"Hey – who the hell do you think *you* are? Leave me alone! Get your hands off me, you pig!"

Deidre Evans fought for a while. When she finally focused on his face in the parking lot while walking toward the cruiser, she shrieked.

"Look at your face! Who did that to you? Oh my god – look at his face!" Her high heels had gotten lost somewhere between the bar and the parking lot. She tried to kick him in the shin, but the attempt was pathetic. He prayed she wouldn't vomit in his cruiser.

Nick imagined he looked awful. The purple bruises around his eyes and his swollen nose was a sight to behold. He mentally reminded himself to use the ice pack in the cruiser after dropping Deidre off. She'd be out in a few hours, once she sobered up. She'd then promise to be the best mother on the planet. Little Henry would be back in her care. That word was a misnomer ~ *care*. He knew how this would play out. And, from the information he gleaned from his iPad in the cruiser, this wasn't the first time she'd left Henry alone.

As he slipped Deidre gently into the backseat of his cruiser, he adjusted the seatbelt around her and clicked it into place. A gob of spit landed on his cheek.

"You're a pig! I hate you!"

She looked like his mom in her heyday and smelled like her, too. She was a rum drinker, just like his mother, God rest her soul. If only she knew what she was doing to that innocent little boy -- he could tell her, but she'd never understand. She was too self-centered to even realize there was a little boy in her life. And, no matter what he said right now, she'd never remember it. She was too drunk.

"Unit 12 heading to County jail to drop off intoxicated female; child endangerment." Nick communicated to dispatch. "Will be back in service shortly."

The rest of the night was filled with traffic stops, a burglary in progress, and a group of young people openly distributing drugs in Bubba's parking lot after the place closed. All in all, nothing out of the ordinary. When midnight came, he rolled into the small building that housed the 38 police officers who barely kept Cherryfield from anarchy and chaos. The midnight shift was coming on for roll-call. He finished his notes and took his gear out of the patrol car and headed for the locker room.

He met his replacement in the hallway, Dan Cooper, and he softly punched him in the shoulder.

"You all set?"

"Yup. You're a good note-taker, Nick. You would've made a good secretary, but damn you'd look ugly in a skirt." Cooper laughed.

"Yeah, I know. I'm the original Neanderthal knuckle-dragger. Shit, I'll be glad when my bruises clear up."

"I heard about that, Nick. I'm sorry. It happens to all of us, you know."

"I blame myself, Coop. I shouldn't have gone after the guy like that. I lost sight of him for a moment. Wasn't thinking. My Neanderthal brain was in hunt mode."

Nick waved goodbye and exited the building. Riding the Harley at night was a special pleasure and he took the long way home through the east side of Cherryfield where pretty little bungalows were perched on a hill overlooking the valley below. Although the lights twinkled in the valley and looked lovely at midnight, that was the tough part of town. But then, lots of things looked better in the dark.

He revved the throttle and cruised past Grace's tiny yellow house. It was cute all right, just like her. *Aw shit. What was he thinking? A woman like that would never want anything to do with him.* Damn fine, she was, giving him meatballs and running her fingers through his hair. How he longed for a relationship like that – one where he didn't do all the giving, but got something in return. It was all he ever wanted, but it seemed to elude him.

At age 28, it was high time he found a female, settled down and got married. If he ever wanted to have a woman like her, he'd need to work on self-improvement. Losing weight, eating better, for starters. Maybe working harder or smarter to be a better cop and someday get promoted. It was important to him to make a difference as a police officer. He didn't want to rise to a leadership position for the glory, but to utilize his abilities to help other officers. He loved the challenge he had before him, one of the greatest on the planet -- to convince those on the wrong path to move toward a productive life.

His cell phone vibrated as he kicked the stand out from under the Harley. He slipped the phone out of his chest pocket and noticed it was Kristie again. He read her text. *I'll be there in a few minutes, baby.* Nick took a deep breath, as he fortified himself for Kristie's visit.

He was in the shower when he heard the knock on his door. In a two-room apartment he could pretty much hear everything. Kristie had repeatedly asked him for a key, but he wasn't about to get in that deep with her. Truth was, he didn't trust her.

"Be right there." Still dripping, Nick wrapped a towel around him and squinted through the peep hole. Kristie was dolled up in a tight gold dress with her hands on her hips.

"Come on, Nicky. I ain't got all night."

As he opened the door, she almost fell into the room. Those damned heels had to be three inches at least.

"Aw, Nicky…your face." Nick felt her hand trace along his jawline as her eyes took in the ugly bruises. "Let me make it better…I knew you were takin' a shower…"

Her hands reached for the towel as her high-heeled foot kicked the door closed. Nick allowed her to push him onto the unmade bed. Her perfume was strong and the smell of alcohol was on her hands, in her clothing. Being a bartender, she always smelled that way.

Kristie sat atop him and pulled her dress over her head with one swift move. His eyes were drawn to her breasts straining against a lacy red bra. She reached back and unhooked it. He was already hard, because he knew what would happen next. Her golden hair fell upon him as she leaned down to place her rosy lips on his. Her kiss was like the soldering heat that joined metal. His tongue danced with hers in a savage intensity. Then, as always, Kristie put him into a trance of divine ecstasy. Slowly, she kissed his chest, then his abdomen and he felt her grab his manhood with both hands. He turned to view them in a full-length mirror against the wall. Her hands were doing things to him, wild things. He became mesmerized with the vision of Kristie stroking, kissing -- and then taking him into her talented mouth. Any sense of reason he ever had seemed to dissipate. He made no attempt to hide the fact that he was watching her. As his heart hammered against his ribs, Kristie stopped and glanced up at him.

"Does this feel good, babe?"

He could barely speak. "Yeah. Yeah."

"You want more?" She teased.

"Yes, more."

Kristie ran her finger along his abdomen.

"You're hot, Nicky. I mean really hot."

She knew what she was doing. He just wondered how many guys she did it with. His brain ceased thinking and focused on needs, desires, impulses. His hand moved down to her head and he allowed his fingers to get lost in her hair.

He whispered, "Do it, baby."

A flash of desire sprang from her eyes as she peered into his. Her head moved between his legs and he inhaled sharply as her mouth tortured him with erotic pleasure. Hypnotized by her seduction, he cried out as she drained him. It was only 1:00 AM. This was how it began. Kristie curled up on his chest and ran her fingers over his eagle tattoo.

"I love this, Nicky."

After he caught his breath, he rolled over and moved above Kristie.

"You're gonna love this, too, then." He rolled the condom on.

All the stress of the night melted away when he thrust himself into Kristie's soft pink center and she wrapped her legs around him. He gave her all that he could as she panted and howled.

"Give it to me, Nicky. Yes!"

He felt her fingernails clawing his back. Kristie knew how to trigger this in him. It was as if she had the power to control him. She knew how to make him crave immediate gratification. It was like this from the very beginning. The first time with Kristie was in the men's room where she tended bar. She'd followed him into the restroom at closing time and pushed him against the wall where she promptly unzipped his fly and fell to her knees. He'd been flirting with her all night, but he never expected *that*.

Once she finished her first orgasm, Kristie collapsed in a heap atop him, and always whined for water or something to eat. Then, in a matter of ten minutes, she'd be ready for him again. After the third time, Nick was spent. Sleep was necessary.

Kristie had a habit of wrapping herself around his back and putting her lips against his ear.

"Can I ask you something?"

Nick pulled the blanket over himself and yawned. "Sure."

"How come you never say you love me?"

Nick kept his eyes closed. Sometimes Kristie would get into this mood, and he wished she would just go home and let him crash. But he knew he had to say something nice to her. After all, she had just performed the most intimate act with him, more than once. She was expecting a kind word.

"Yes. It was great, babe. I loved it."

"Okay." Kristie rolled away and he sensed her disappointment. Through half closed eyes he watched her as she dressed in the mirror.

"Nicky, can you take a look at my car? The brakes need work. I thought you were gonna do it today."

"Sure. I'll look at it."

"Later, babe." The door closed and she was gone. Nick exhaled. He wondered if Kristie was a nymphomaniac. He began to worry that these nightly romps were becoming too routine. Kristie wanted more than he could give. Yes, he enjoyed the physical sensations she provided. But afterward, there was always the same feeling, a letdown. Instead of cuddling with her, he wanted just the opposite. He'd be fine if she'd skip the clinging routine and slip away. But then, Kristie was trying to forge a relationship and he was just enjoying the sex. It had sort of evolved into a quid pro quo. She gave him sex and he worked on her car. She gave him sex and he painted her apartment. He never said no to Kristie. He couldn't. He never told her he loved her; he tried to justify that as being truthful. But he knew deep down, it really didn't fly.

He retrieved the ice pack from the freezer and put it on his pillow with a towel over it, then buried his face into it until his head felt numb. It quelled the physical pain, but the emptiness he felt inside could not be dulled. Kristie was the least of his worries right now. Beth was calling him and texting, too. Even though she was cute, he knew sleeping with her was a mistake. She was Kristie's friend and it was only a matter of time before one would find out about the other.

Why was he able to be strong and tough when it came to taking down a criminal or pushing himself physically on the obstacle course? Then, when it came to women, he surrendered. He rarely made a move on a chick, they always came to him. Other guys joked he had it made. But, often he laid back and enjoyed the carnal pleasure just because he could. Truth was, none of those women meant anything to him. A therapist would've had fun with the implications of it all.

He fell asleep on the ice pack and his face was cool when he woke in the morning. The towel was wet, ice melted, but the bruising had begun its fading process. When he looked into the mirror to shave, he noticed the marks had now settled into a combination of green and purple. His nose, however, was still swollen and tender to touch. More ice today.

Chapter 5

Paco waited in the back of the parking lot at Bud's Diner for Nick to show up. A text had appeared asking him to meet behind the dumpster. One of the security lights was out and it was blacker than usual. For this, Paco was grateful. He didn't want anyone seeing him talking to a cop. Diesel was by his side as he sat against the building in the darkness. The patrol car rolled around the corner slowly and moved across the back of the parking lot, then pulled closer and Paco approached.

"Get in. I need to talk with you about something." Nick nodded toward the empty front seat. "You can put Diesel in the back."

"I'll sit in the back with him." Paco said.

Nick took Paco on a short ride diagonally across the street to a storage facility.

"I patrol through here."

"Yeah, I know." Paco answered.

"The young couple running this storage business are moving to Florida. They asked me if I knew anyone who might want to take this over. See that little house right there? They live in it. It's only 400 square feet, but it's a home. The book work is fairly simple. Are you interested?"

Paco rubbed the stubble on his chin. He was shocked Nick thought he was capable enough to do a job. He doubted anyone would hire a homeless veteran with PTSD and a methadone habit. But then, he knew he needed to do something before winter arrived. It was Nick's idea or the shelter.

"Can I keep Diesel with me?"

"Yes. I asked about that. The owner of the place said he'd actually prefer to have a dog on the premises. This place gets broken into sometimes."

"One more question." Paco took a deep breath. "You think they'd hire someone like me?"

"Yeah. I do. I already told the owner about you. He wants to meet you and Diesel. But, I've got to get you a bit more… presentable. I've got a friend about your size and he's tossing out some shirts and pants that will probably fit you. I can schedule a haircut and a shave for you, too. What do you say?"

"Can I ask one more question?" Paco looked away as they drove back to Bud's Diner.

"Sure."

"Why're you being so nice to me?"

"Because, you're a veteran. You served this country. You shouldn't be living like this, Paco. If you think I'm crazy, that's okay. Take the job and maybe you'll be in a position to help someone out in the future. That's what it's all about, man, doing some good. That's why I got into law enforcement."

Paco slipped out of the car with Diesel by his side. He scanned the area nervously. Nick handed him an iPhone.

"The department gave us new ones. This one was my personal phone. I wiped it. It's yours."

"Hey, thanks. I mean it." Paco felt the words catch in his throat. No one gave a damn about him, ever, except for Diesel…and his brothers in arms.

Nick waved him off.

"I'll meet you here tomorrow in the daytime at Noon. I'll bring clothes, and I'll drop you off at Discount Haircuts. There's a girl there. She cuts my hair. It's all set up."

"Hey ~ how'd you know I'd say yes?" Paco squinted suspiciously into Nick's eyes.

"I just had a feeling." Nick smiled.

The cruiser pulled away and Paco waited, then rummaged through the dumpster. The good stuff wasn't in there yet. He looked at his phone. In a few minutes, George would be coming out back to toss the stuff from the refrigerator so he could start fresh in the morning. Paco leaned against the building hidden in the shadows.

He watched a black Lexus SUV pull into a motel parking lot. Two men, dressed in black, got out of the vehicle as a gold Chrysler mini-van pulled up behind them. Paco had a good view and snapped photos with his new phone. He was thankful Nick had given him the iPhone. This device took great photos even with fluorescent lighting at the back of the motel. He noticed the bright lights made the license plates perfectly legible. The motel had been a hot spot for drug activity and arrests in the last year. Paco had watched them all from afar, but now he could participate in getting them locked up. He'd seen their handiwork in the neighborhood and throughout the state. The way they sucked the life out of people was grotesque, inhuman. And, he wondered if these guys even *had* a soul. Their love of money replaced any love they ever had for fellow human beings. Dealers were nothing more than monsters to him.

The door to Bud's kitchen opened to the right of him. He scurried to see if he could get the food before George tossed it into the dumpster in the paper sack.

"Hey, Paco. How're you tonight?" George handed him a paper bag filled with food.

"Thanks, George."

"Aw, get out of here before the cops come by."

Paco tucked the bag under his arm as if it were filled with gold.

"Yes, sir. You have a good night."

As Paco made his way back to the ravine, he got a better look at the men who appeared to be making a drug transaction in the parking lot. Diesel trotted obediently next to him with his nose in the air as he tried to catch the aroma escaping from the bag.

In the ravine, Paco got comfortable in the tent and made a fire. The wool blanket Grace had given him was a lifesaver that night. He covered up with Diesel after they'd eaten a delicious meal. For the first time, Paco realized George had been making these meals deliberately for him. Plastic forks and knives were tucked into napkins and he always included condiments in little packets.

He nervously contemplated what tomorrow would be like. He hadn't worn clean clothes for a long time. And getting a haircut and a shave filled him with anxiety. What if the owner of the storage place didn't want him? He tried to ignore the negative thoughts that invaded his mind. Paco and Diesel fell asleep and the fire burned down to a few hot coals.

* * *

Nick woke to the sound of his alarm and pulled on a sweatshirt and jeans. While brushing his teeth and splashing cold water on his face, he thought about last night and Kristie. She had already sent him two texts and a voice message, which he had yet to listen to. He had to admit, she was wild and fun in the sack, but he couldn't shake the sinking feeling afterward. As he examined his face in the mirror, he was horrified to think he'd become one of those guys who used women.

He always hated the guys who had treated his mother that way, used her for sex then disappeared. He remembered how she got herself emotionally attached the first night she'd kiss a man, and how it tortured her when he'd never return after the bedroom gymnastics. He often wondered if her hunger for love was behind her alcohol addiction. He wasn't sure what fueled her craving for it, but he did know he didn't want to be one of those guys – the one who treated a woman like a piece of human garbage. He made a silent promise to be honest with Kristie and with Beth. It would be better to make a clean break than to drag it on and hurt them like that. He needed to be truthful.

He tossed the suitcase filled with freshly laundered clothing into the back of the Jeep, thankful for Cooper's donation. When he saw the clothing ready to be sent to the thrift store in Cooper's vehicle, Nick told Cooper he had a friend in need. Sunlight streamed through the windshield as he drove over to Bud's Diner. Hell, he practically lived at the place. It made no sense to cook meals in his apartment. When he figured it out, eating at Bud's was actually cheaper than grocery shopping and cooking. As he opened the glass door, his favorite waitress, Naomi, usurped the authority of the receptionist and led him to his usual table for two in the corner of her section.

"Hey, blue eyes. How're you this mornin'?"

Her voice had a little tinge of southern. Nick loved the way she spoiled him. She wrapped her long dark hair around her finger when she spoke. Although she flirted with him, she seemed a little shy.

"What's on your agenda today, Officer Kozlovsky?"

"Oh, something good and hot to eat, like your super omelet and a side of bacon and home fries." Nick never looked at the menu. He knew what he wanted to eat before he got there. Naomi brought him coffee and cream. When she turned away he felt her eyes lingering. She was attractive, yes. And, she knew just how to wiggle that shapely ass of hers when she turned to walk away. But she was friends with his younger sister, Sophia, and 19 was way too young for him.

When she brought the food, Nick asked, "Hey – have you seen Sophia lately?"

"No. Actually, I was going to ask you if she'd changed jobs or something." Naomi wrinkled her brow. "Last time I had my car washed, she was the cashier, but she told me she was looking for something better. She mentioned working at Stop 'N Shop, maybe."

Nick put a forkful of the steaming omelet with melted cheese, peppers, and onions into his mouth while he listened to Naomi. He pulled out his phone and tapped Sophia's number, but it rang and went to her voicemail. That was the fourth time he'd called her in the last two days. He made a mental note to check in with Lexi, Sophia's best friend.

But first, it was time to pick up Paco and get him though his one-day makeover. The next few hours were spent with an anxiety-ridden Paco and his hungry dog. Nick brought him to the gym and insisted he take a proper shower. Then Nick sat on the bench in the locker room while Paco tried on the gently used clothing. Nick was a bit surprised when Paco removed his shirt and he saw the large tattoo of an Eagle. Oddly, the tattoo was an exact replica of the one that adorned Nick's chest.

"Hey, it's none of my business, but where did you get that tattoo?" Nick asked.

"Oh, this? A guy named Billy Bob Goodman. He has that place on Spring Street, you know, the tattoo parlor, oh what's the name of it – Tits and Tats. Yeah, that's it."

"No kidding? I got mine there, too." Nick said, astonished. "Same damn one!"

"Huh, that's funny. Why'd you get yours? I got mine just before I went to Afghanistan. My name, Paco, the meaning is Eagle. I'm Native American and Hispanic, but thought it would be appropriate, you know?"

"Yeah. I got mine in college. I'm an eagle boy scout and patriotic as hell."

Paco smiled and Nick grinned. "Yeah, I guess we're brothers after all."

Once Paco tried on a pair of khaki pants with a light blue shirt and a gray jacket, Nick packed up the rest of the clothing. "That's it. You look ready for a job interview."

Paco's anxiety seemed at its highest when Susan cut his hair and trimmed his beard.

"I want a little bit of facial hair; you know? I'm used to it." Paco asserted.

Susan made him look like a male model. Nick was stunned by the transformation.

When Paco looked at himself in the mirror, he whispered, "Man, is that *me*?"

"Don't you like it?" Nick pulled him out of the shop. "Come on, we've got an appointment."

He left a good tip for Susan and waved goodbye. Diesel got a handful of dog biscuits as they drove into the parking lot of the storage facility.

"Take a deep breath, and let it out slowly." Nick winked at Paco. "You'll do fine."

When he knocked on the door, Nick noticed Paco's hand was shaking.

"Sorry, I'm nervous." Paco whispered.

After a thirty-minute interview with Bob Wilson and a tour of the place, Paco signed some paperwork and was a newly hired employee.

"Here's the big question." Wilson rose from his chair. "Can you start right away?"

Nick saw the look of joy on Paco's face for the first time since he'd seen him.

"Sure."

The manager told Paco to be there tomorrow at 9 AM, he'd get the keys and a password for the computer. He handed Paco a booklet explaining medical benefits and the standard operating procedures, which were fairly straightforward. Even Diesel wagged his tail.

Nick dropped Paco off at the ravine with a suitcase full of clothes and $20.

"Hey, take care, Paco. I'll be in touch." Nick gestured to his phone.

"Yeah. I've got some video for you from last night." Paco handed Nick his phone.

Nick played the video on Paco's phone and e-mailed it to himself. Then deleted it from Paco's.

"Wow, thanks. I'll pass this on, anonymously."

As Nick drove away from Paco, his missing sister became the focus of his attention for the remainder of his day. He stopped by the car wash, but the manager said Sophia had quit a week ago. He went into the Stop 'N Shop, but they said she hadn't made an application. He'd already called his brothers Victor and Alex and they said they hadn't heard from her. Katie, 17 and Julia, 15 were still in high school. They didn't run with the same crowd Sophia did. But he checked with them anyway. They mentioned her Facebook page hadn't had any posts recently. He checked it out and they were right.

At that moment, a thought occurred to him. Lexi could be the key to Sophia's whereabouts. She knew the crowd Sophia ran with. He'd picked up one of Lexi's friends a few days ago. Her name was Taylor and she was high. Taylor was a year older than Sophia and Lexi. Nick remembered her working at the car wash, too. She was dating some ex-con who worked there. He was covered with gang tattoos. Nick's brow wrinkled and he closed his eyes. *Please, don't let her be mixed up with that posse.*

Lately Nick had noticed some disturbing things. Taylor was spending too much time in barroom parking lots. She was beautiful but still only 20. She'd found ways to get alcohol and anything else she needed. Nick busted her while giving guys sex in the parking lot in exchange for synthetic marijuana. Unlike the homegrown stuff of years ago, the chemical concoction known as Molly could be deadly. The chemicals in it kept a human brain on high alert all day and all night, right up to the point of hallucinations.

Nick took a turn and headed for the county jail. As far as he knew, Taylor might still be there. She had no money, no way of making bail. But when he got there, the bailiff told him she was out. She'd been picked up by a guy by the name of Jason Dennis.

It was nearly 2:30 PM, time for him to get ready for his shift. He raced to the station and prepped in the locker room for roll call. As Officer Stevens walked by, Nick nudged him.

"Hey, remember that chick we busted a week ago – Taylor?"

"Yeah, why."

"She got bailed out by some dude named Jason Dennis. You know him?"

"Yeah. He's a dealer. Heroin and Oxy…synthetic marijuana. He's a New York boy."

"No shit. Where's he holed up?"

"He moves around quite a bit. You'll have to check with the detectives. They're probably tailing him. He leads them to all sorts of low-life crap. See you in roll call."

Nick wiped his brow and grabbed his vest and gear. *Heroin.* That's the last thing he wanted to hear. Heroin and Oxy were sweeping the state of Connecticut killing young people faster than a life-threatening plague. After roll call, he passed the video Paco gave him off to the detectives. He mentioned he was looking for Taylor and Jason Dennis. Oh yeah, and his sister, Sophia. He casually mentioned Sophia's name. They assured him he'd be contacted if they could locate any of them.

As Nick walked away from the detectives, he imagined they were wondering why he didn't know where his own sister was. Right now, he was thinking the same thing. What cop lets his own family member roam with wolves? He hated himself for wasting time with Kristie and Beth when he could've been checking up on his vulnerable sister. Yeah. Great protector he was. Frustration, anger, and shame ran through him as he walked toward his cruiser.

As soon as he navigated his car to the edge of the parking lot, the dispatcher called.

"Unit 12, to a domestic on 25 Valley Street. Report of shots fired. Calling back-up."

"Unit 12 on the way." Nick spoke into the mic as he switched on the lights and siren. He hated domestic calls more than anything. He'd prefer to break up a fight in Bubba's parking lot or face down a whole gang of drug dealers. Nothing got to him more than some asshole beating his wife and kids, and that was usually the situation he'd roll up on. He steeled himself for the worst.

When he arrived on the scene he hadn't imagined the worst. On his portable radio, he heard Officer Herrick on his way. But Nick didn't hesitate. He bolted out of his cruiser and leaned his body against the side of the house to avoid detection. Inside the ramshackle multi-unit dwelling Nick heard bloodcurdling screams, coming from a female. When he stepped onto the porch he scooted along the wall to the doorway to the first-floor unit. The view from the porch window gave him plenty of information. A woman was crouched over a tiny figure on the floor, there was blood. No time to waste. He tried to open the door but it was bolted shut. He knocked on the door with his baton.

"Police! Open the door." Nick heard footsteps and a scuffling sound inside, but the door remained locked.

He stepped back and kicked it open, holding his revolver in his right hand.

"He killed my baby!" the woman wailed.

"Where is he?" Nick asked. No answer.

Herrick's siren sounded like he was on the front lawn.

Nick turned and thought he heard footsteps outside, on the porch. When he got to the window, he saw the suspect fleeing into the backyard through clotheslines filled with laundry, sheds, fences, garbage cans. Nick spoke briefly into his handheld radio.

"Foot pursuit backyard 25 Valley Street. Not sure if suspect is armed. Get a wagon here."

Instinctively, Nick had already started running. Adrenaline propelled him toward the fleeing man. He never let him out of his line of sight, even though he moved around a tree and climbed a fence, Nick was closing in on him – the distance minimized to the point where he could see the man's face as he looked over his shoulder. The suspect stumbled. He didn't appear to be armed. Nick holstered his weapon, reached for his handcuffs and was on him.

With his knee in the suspect's back, Nick cuffed the young dark-skinned man who was yelling words at him in another language. Nick frisked him and found nothing. He was barefoot. Several neighbors were now gathered around.

"Where's the gun?" Nick asked him, as his heart beat against his ribs. No answer.

"Why are you taking him?" a rotund woman with a brightly colored scarf tied around her face yelled at him. Then another female pushed him, but Nick held the man captive and pressed toward the cruiser. Other young people surrounded him in the driveway. Officer Herrick was radioing for back-up. The woman was still wailing and Nick knew the little girl she held in her arms was dead. The woman holding the dead child couldn't be more than a teenager herself. But the man in handcuffs was in his thirties at least. Others in the crowd of ten or twelve people started hitting Nick with bottles, rocks, and one had a baseball bat.

Officer Herrick made an attempt to quell the crowd, and he sent a worried glance Nick's way.

"Find the perp's gun." Nick growled as he hustled the suspect to his cruiser, put him into the backseat and shut the door. The crowd had swelled to twenty or more. Rocks and other objects struck his cruiser and Nick was hit with a baseball bat. That's when he turned on them. Something happened. He stifled the strong instinct to strike back. But his voice was commanding as it rose from his chest to his throat.

"Get out of here now, all of you! If you hit me again, you're going to jail with him!"

His voice resonated above the shouts of the people. *They were chanting something about pigs – police must die. Kill the police. For a split second, Nick wanted to take the baton to all of them. Didn't they know he had a murderer in his cruiser? One of their own was a murderer? He'd killed a girl. Apparently, their hatred for cops surpassed that.*

Officer Herrick called out to him. "Get out of here with him, Nick. I've got two other officers coming. They'll be here in a few minutes, along with the ambulance – although, I don't think we need it. We need the coroner."

"I'll make the call." Nick glared at the crowd surrounding his patrol car once again. He didn't want to hit a bystander, although they really couldn't be called that now. They were inciting violence.

"Get away!" Nick waved his arm. He slid into the cruiser and turned on the lights and siren. The crowd parted, but not before a cinderblock crashed through the cruiser's back window and Nick shook his head as he gazed in the rearview mirror.

The man in the backseat laughed. He glared at Nick for the whole ride to the county jail.

As Nick took him out of the cruiser, he recited Miranda rights.

"You have the right to remain silent…"

"Yeah, I know." Now his prisoner spoke English.

"I have to inform you of your rights. I'm required by law to do this."

Nick looked into the man's red-rimmed eyes. Yes, he was a drug-user. The tracks on his arms gave him away. He'd even had tattoos placed so they'd not be so noticeable. None of that mattered now. He'd killed a girl. At least that would be the charge. Nick finished his spiel and walked the suspect with a sour attitude into the processing area. The man threatened to sue him. He wanted an attorney. The man in custody had become surly and sullen as he leaned in close to Nick.

"I'll have your badge ~ you son-of-a-bitch."

Nick did not respond. After filling out what seemed like endless paperwork, Nick slid back into his cruiser. The blood of the man's feet had run onto the mats in the back. Once again, the radio dictated his actions.

"Unit 12 there's a disturbance in an abandoned house on Spring Street, Number 44. Multiple units responding."

The dispatcher put the call out to all available. Nick floored the accelerator and ran a couple of red lights. He was six blocks from the scene so he was first to arrive. Plywood protected the windows of the house, and graffiti covered the plywood. This address had a reputation for drug addicts and homeless derelicts and he waited in his cruiser for back-up to appear. Like the cavalry, they arrived, lights blazing, sirens blasting. Two younger officers breached the door which was piled high with trash and broken furniture. In the corner were two young girls sleeping on a stained mattress. The smell of meth cooking was overwhelming. His eyes traveled over the scene. *What disturbance?* These people were so high, they couldn't even stand up, let alone speak. His eyes darted to the back window as the figure of a fleeing man whizzed by and two officers closed in on him.

Then he noticed a young woman on the back porch in a fetal position. Matted blonde hair covered her face and her clothing reeked of urine. As he touched her shoulder, she winced as if she was in pain. Nick spoke to her, wondering if she was even alive.

"Miss, are you all right?"

When her face turned toward him, he could see the glassy-eyed stare, and his heart nearly stopped beating. "Taylor!"

He slipped his arms beneath her slender body. Her limbs flopped clumsily in every direction. She'd passed out. Nick couldn't stop the thoughts racing through his mind. Sophia's friend was possibly dying in his arms. He had Narcan in his cruiser and raced alongside the house with her limp body in his arms to get to it. He laid her in the backseat of his car as he rummaged through the trunk and found the injectable dose. When he pulled up her skirt, he slapped her face gently.

"Taylor, tell me what you took. Just say it."

"Heroin." She whispered.

Her vitals were failing. She was down to less than 50 for a pulse and he watched as her eyes rolled up and her lids closed. Nick wrapped the blood pressure cuff around her arm. Her pressure was dropping dangerously low. Nick pulled her skirt higher and wiped her thigh with alcohol, then thrust the needle in. He had a bottle of cold water in his cruiser and brought it to her as he held her in his arms.

"Taylor. Look at me." His voice was loud, firm, but he felt terror run through him.

He shook her gently and her head rolled to one side.

"Leave me alone." She murmured.

For the next sixty seconds, he dabbed cold water on her face, called her name, and she started to respond. Taylor's eyes opened and she seemed to be getting her bearings.

"What happened?"

"I'm taking you for a ride. Relax."

He belted her into the front seat and raced to the emergency room. His hand automatically touched the siren and lights as he called to the hospital through dispatch.

"Unit 12 bringing possible overdose patient to Cherryfield Emergency Room."

Cherryfield ER responded. "Name, vitals, what do you have?"

"Her name is Taylor Thomas, she's 20 years of age, her heart rate was 50, overdose of heroin suspected, she told me she injected heroin just before she passed out. Administered Narcan. She's conscious now."

"10-4 Unit 12. We're ready."

Nick slowed down at the red lights, and luckily traffic moved to the side. Often cars just stopped in the middle of the road making his job all the harder. But tonight, everything seemed to fall into place and within minutes he was handing Taylor over to the ER staff. He waited patiently in the reception area.

The doctor emerged and told him it would be a while. Once examined and admitted, Taylor would be handed off to the emergency room team and monitored closely.

"No need to stay right now. Her vitals are good, but we need to do lots of tests to find out how much damage has been done by the drugs. You said it was heroin. Do you know if she uses anything else?" The doctor waited for an answer, but Nick didn't have one.

The doctor pressed him. "Do you have a phone number for her parents?"

Nick found the phone number and gave it to him.

"I'll call them." The doctor turned away. Nick had the feeling he'd run through this scenario many times -- too many.

The last image he carried was that of Taylor's ravaged body lying beneath a sheet and a blanket in the ER cubicle. She couldn't have weighed more than 100 pounds, and she was five foot seven. He wondered how anyone could waste away so quickly. He'd only seen her a short time ago and she appeared healthy, although he remembered she looked tired.

When he got back into the patrol car, he exhaled and spoke to dispatch.

"Unit 12, 10-8, back in service. My car has a broken window. Will return to station for replacement."

After putting his gear into the replacement cruiser, he headed through the Bermuda Triangle and realized he hadn't eaten anything for six hours. The thought of eating hadn't occurred to him. But he wasn't too far from Bud's. He could swing by and grab something to take out to his cruiser. So much for cutting back on calories. Comfort food, that's what he craved right now, and a BLT with a side of fries would fill him up. He fingered his phone and tapped the number for Bud's. His order would be ready when he arrived and he washed with the disposable antibacterial wipes before heading inside.

Chapter 6

Grace Robertson had been trying on clothes for her Labor Day weekend getaway. She had to purchase a wetsuit and found one on sale. It would be an all-girl adventure. She realized it wasn't important what she wore. She'd only bring the essentials in her backpack. The focus of the trip was to have fun, relax – something she hadn't done in a long time. She stopped at the grocer's and stocked up on her favorite granola bars, trail mix and a large stainless-steel water bottle with a strap.

After going to the bank and dry cleaners, her stomach growled and she realized she hadn't eaten all day. Pulling into Bud's diner, the early evening crowd was starting to arrive. Gray-haired couples and families with young children filled the reception area. Grace hated eating alone, but the nice receptionist tucked her in a corner table for two, out of the way. From there she had a good view of the entire room. She glanced through the menu, but what she really wanted wasn't on it. *She wanted a man.* Not a married one like Michael Dean. She wanted a real man, honest, truthful, someone who made her laugh. And, he had to be sexy, too.

Her eyes drifted above the menu and there he was, Nick Kozlovsky. For a second she felt like her wish had been granted. He was being handed a takeout meal from the waitress and she was gushing over him. *Who wouldn't?* He was so damned cute, yet he seemed oblivious to that fact. Just before he turned to leave, his gaze came to rest on her questioning eyes and he strode to her table. *Oh damn, everyone in the place turned to watch the handsome police officer as he approached her table.*

"Hey, Grace. How're you tonight?"

She instantly blushed and cursed herself for doing so. "Good. I'm getting dinner."

Oh wow, that sounded lame. Of course, she was getting dinner.

"Me, too. I'm in a rush here, on duty. But I wanted to tell you -- I never got the chance to thank you for being so kind the other night in the ER. I'm sorry I wasn't on my best behavior."

Nick had removed his hat during this conversation and tucked it under his arm. Grace couldn't remember the last time she'd seen a guy do that. There was something humble about him, endearing. Her first reaction was to stand up and run her fingers through his hair, ask him if he was feeling better.

"Your bruises are not as bad. Still have some color around your eyes." *Argh. She chastised herself for being so damned medical.*

"Hey, look, I've gotta go. But, thank you – for being *you*."

He turned around and she watched him exit the building. A few other women did the same. She had a hot flash right there remembering that moment when she ran her hand over his chest and his arms in the ER and snuck a peak at his rear when he turned. Several diners gazed her way and she felt her face warm to a deep shade of pink. Something about Officer Nick intrigued her. Yes, her body reacted involuntarily when she was near him. That pull was strong. But it was so much more than butterflies she was feeling. His presence filled her with joy.

Tonight, however, his face didn't seem filled with joy, but concern. And he seemed to be in a hurry. She wondered what he was doing out there in the darkness. What was his night shift like? She had a rough idea. The patrolmen often dropped off victims of crime in the ER while she was there. Quite a few lives were saved by their quick timing. They made life and death decisions on a regular basis. That was something she had in common with them.

Tonight she'd volunteered to swap shifts with one of the other doctors; she'd go in at midnight and get out at 7 AM. She finished her meal, but couldn't stop thinking about Nick Kozlovsky. While eating, she picked up her phone and googled his name. She found lots of interesting articles. As a first-year cop, he'd broken the record for rookie arrests. His Facebook page had photographs of motorcycles, especially the blue one. He also posted articles on policing, psychology, crime statistics, criminal justice in general. No photos of family or a girlfriend that she could discern. He had hundreds of followers, mostly female. *That wasn't a good sign.* Then she remembered. One of the other policemen had mentioned once that cops never put photos of family members on their Facebook page, due to death threats. In fact, not many law enforcement guys even *had* a Facebook page.

She was impressed with the work he'd done with the local Boy Scout troop. He was an eagle scout, himself, and had been a scout master for a couple of years. She took a deep breath and sighed – a Boy Scout and a police officer. She'd dated quite a few guys, but she'd never run across anyone quite like Nick. She clicked on the friend request button and closed her eyes for a moment. He'd recognize her name immediately. *Would he think she was stalking him?* She sent the request anyway.

Grace gazed at the full moon when she stepped outside of the diner. What would it be like to be on a date with Nick Kozlovsky? He was single, she was single. There was no reason to say no, if he asked her. *But would he ask her?*

As she hummed along with a tune on the radio while driving home, she realized she had been working too much. It was fun to have these quiet moments to think of things besides work. Labor Day weekend couldn't come quickly enough for her. Laughing with her friends was what she needed more than anything right now.

She pulled her hair into a pony tail and folded her neatly pressed white jacket over her arm. As she checked herself in the mirror near the doorway, she tried to imagine what it might be like to kiss Nick. She pouted in the mirror and puckered up.

She liked her lips, they were one of her more feminine features. Nick had full lips, for a guy, and always smelled like motor oil and fresh air. Then, almost instantly, she allowed herself to fall into a black hole of negativity.

What could he possibly see in her? She was a workaholic and had a long tempestuous affair with a married man. She was a geek. At least that's what Michael had called her. She didn't want to think about Michael right now, or ever, really. But, he kept haunting her thoughts, especially when she pondered loving someone again. Would it really be worth it to put herself out there and possibly get her heart broken, or worse, be used for erotic pleasure by a guy who couldn't commit?

But she kept telling herself, she couldn't go on like this – living alone. She was becoming a recluse -- a cat lady, minus the cats.

* * *

Nick Kozlovsky finished his shift with an assault and battery call, then realized it was almost midnight. He had twenty minutes before he'd need to brief his replacement. He wanted to check on Taylor in the ER. As he pulled into the hospital parking lot, he noticed the Land Rover pulling into the reserved space. He stood next to his cruiser in the darkness. He thought for a moment about going in, making some excuse to see Grace in the ER, but then he reconsidered. He'd already spoken to her in the diner. Hell, he didn't want Grace to think he was stalking her, but he did notice her friend request on Facebook. She was thinking about him. That was a good sign. After checking on Taylor, he slipped into his patrol car and exited the lot. One more drive-by -- to check on Paco.

At the ravine, he stopped his Jeep, stepped out and peered down. Paco had a fire going and his faithful canine was there with him. *This would be his last night homeless.* Nick smiled. He didn't want to disturb them. He thought about Paco sleeping in a real bed and Diesel having a place to stay tomorrow. *This was the one thing in his life that truly brought him joy – helping someone in need.*

He drove the Jeep into the driveway of his dilapidated apartment building and parked in the back. Inside, he showered as was his habit when he got off shift. He still had Taylor in the back of his mind, and his sister, Sophia. He couldn't imagine he had missed the signs. His thoughts shifted to his other young siblings. Katie and Julia had been living with Aunt Brenda since their mother died. They planned to room together in an apartment once they finished high school. Both girls were in the running for a scholarship. Serious students, both of them. He had no worries there. But, Sophia was a different story. She was the wild one in the family. And, now, for some reason, Nick couldn't stop the awful images that occupied his mind.

Whenever he thought about his childhood, he fell into a dark mood. He blamed it on living alone, and it was probably one of the reasons he welcomed Kristie, Beth, and any warm female body for a pleasurable boost of endorphins. But when he thought about his best friend, Paul, getting married to Amanda, his high school sweetheart and the love of his life, he secretly wished it was him.

He turned on the television and curled up on the bed and closed his eyes. Before falling asleep, he allowed himself to think of the upcoming weekend. Paul was getting married and he had to play some sort of trick on him at this bachelor white water rafting trip. He'd talk to the other guys and they'd cook something up. *Pranks – he lived for that stuff.* Good distraction, playing jokes on one another. It was fun to laugh with his friends because most of his life was filled with encountering human beings at their worst. Arresting people, subduing suspects, stepping into the middle of drunken brawls, heated domestic disputes, dodging bullets, seeing abused children, animals, helpless females, watching addicts destroy their lives ~ riding the adrenaline roller coaster, day in and day out. *The job consumed him.* But, then he had lived his whole life to be in this role. And, his early years equipped him well for whatever the job could throw at him.

* * *

In the morning, Paco worked quickly as he sorted through his belongings. He was amazed at how much stuff he'd accumulated in the six months he'd lived in the ravine. After cleaning up in Bud's gas station's rest room, and putting on the clothes Nick had given him, he walked over to Strictly Storage and slid the key into the lock. Mr. Wilson was already there.

"Hello. Come in. I'll show you how the computer system works. Then, I'll be on my way. If you need anything or have questions, you can call me at this number."

Paco listened to everything Mr. Wilson told him and jotted down notes as he spoke. Diesel slurped water from a bowl he'd filled and put in the corner of the room. It was hard to suppress the feelings that ran through him. He hadn't lived inside a dwelling for more than half a year. It felt warm, secure, and for the first time since he'd been home from Afghanistan, he allowed himself to relax a little. His eyes traveled to the small bedroom off the main room. It had been a long time since he'd slept in a real bed. He even had a small kitchen with appliances.

Mr. Wilson shook his hand and left. "Good luck, Paco. And, don't hesitate to call me."

"Thank you, sir." Paco's words caught in his throat. He was crying and hoped that Wilson hadn't noticed. Soldiers weren't supposed to cry.

As soon as the door closed and Paco was alone, he went over every inch of the place. It was clean and neat, and the smell of Lysol lingered. There were dishes in the cupboard and silverware in a drawer. Some food was left in a cabinet. Oatmeal, pasta, and salsa. That would be dinner tonight. Paco opened the bag of dog food and filled Diesel's dish. He could tell the dog was happy. Diesel ate with gusto then hopped onto the sofa with Paco as he touched the remote to turn on the small television. Paco was afraid if he fell asleep, he'd wake and this would all be a dream.

Late that night, Paco saw the patrol car make a pass through the parking lot. He'd left the kitchen light on, hoping he would stop. The vehicle pulled over and Nick hopped out. Paco opened the door.

"Come on in. Take a look!" Paco waved his hand and smiled.

"Wow! This is bigger than my apartment." Nick laughed as he stepped inside and walked around. Paco swelled with pride as his benefactor took in the place, then quickly moved toward the door.

"Thank you, again. I won't forget this." Paco murmured.

"Sleep tight." Nick said as he closed the door. "Text me if you need anything."

Paco watched the door shut and he slid the dead bolt as Nick drove away. There wasn't anything he wouldn't do for Nick Kozlovsky. The officer probably had no idea that he had a friend for life. Paco moved to the bedroom and took his sneakers off. The bed felt like a big soft cloud and he fell asleep immediately. He imagined this was what heaven felt like.

Chapter 7

Grace was thrilled when Friday night's shift finally ended. She cruised in the Land Rover to her bungalow and filled a few canvas bags with what she'd need for the coming weekend. She could barely sleep she was so excited. Awake bright and early Saturday morning, she showered and ate breakfast. Before 8 AM she was on the road. Grace looked forward to scenery and hiking, and viewing waterfalls along the Appalachian Trail. Her destination on the Housatonic River included rustic cabins and an historic covered bridge near the put-in site.

Her phone vibrated and she glanced down at the text sent by her friend, Sarah. *Hope it's okay with you guys, but there'll be a bachelorette party in the other cabins near us. Maybe we'll get a male stripper! That might be wishful thinking.* Grace responded. *That's fine with me. The more, the merrier.* She smiled. Good, there would be other girls sharing the campsite and one was getting married. Lucky, her.

She tapped her phone and the GPS came up with the map to the place. Thank goodness for technology. The electronic voice guided her through the trip and she arrived earlier than Sarah and the others. The cabins were made of cedar logs and nestled into a thickly forested area. Each one had a screened front porch and the key she was given at the office had the number five on it. She parked in a cleared space apart from the cabins, and removed her gear as she inhaled the fresh autumn air.

As Grace got out of her Land Rover, she noticed there was a blue motorcycle there, and several pick-up trucks with big tires. In the back of the trucks were cases of beer. This didn't look much like a bachelorette party. Sarah's voice was behind her.

"Hey, wait up."

Grace stopped walking and Sarah caught up with her, laden with a duffle bag and her purse.

"What number are we?" Sarah asked breathlessly.

"Five. And, by the way – that doesn't look like a bachelorette party to me. Trucks and motorcycles?"

"Well, that's what the owner said." Sarah rolled her eyes.

Rebecca and Ingrid arrived a few minutes later and they caught up to Grace and Sarah. As Grace understood, Saturday would be a hike, then relaxation and a meal by the campfire. That sounded good to her. The girls stowed their gear inside the cabin. Grace plopped in a wooden Adirondack chair and put her feet up on the cooler. It was quiet and only the sound of birds singing and the chatter of the girls in the cabins broke the silence.

"Are you ready to go for a walk?" Grace stretched. "I want to see this place. "Let's go check out the river."

As she uttered the words, a husky figure emerged to her right. He was walking down the gravel path toward them with a purposeful stride. Several guys behind him were carrying racks of beer on their shoulders.

Without his uniform on, Grace recognized him immediately, but couldn't believe her eyes. She stood next to the chair as Nick Kozlovsky approached and stopped right in front of her.

"Well, I didn't expect to see *you* here!" He smiled.

"You guys don't exactly look like a *bachelorette* party." Grace smiled. She was momentarily disarmed by his boyish demeanor. She decided it would be a good idea to introduce him to the girls.

Sarah, Ingrid, and Rebecca all stared at Grace. "You *know* him?"

"Yes, ladies, meet Officer Nick Kozlovsky….and his…friends."

Nick shook their hands and removed his baseball cap, the consummate gentleman.

"Heck, this ain't no bachelorette party, it's a *bachelor's* party. My friend here, Paul, is getting married and white-water rafting was on his bucket list. So, here we are. But we're hiking today. Rafting tomorrow." Nick's smile was handsome.

"Yes. That's what we're doing, too." Grace couldn't take her eyes off him. He wore jeans and a police-issued T-shirt with a Red Sox baseball cap. His well-defined biceps flexed as he carried a duffle bag and a cardboard box filled with food.

Excitement stirred inside of Grace as she stood next to Nick. It was as if she thought about him and he appeared. This was the second time that happened.

"Well, you girls don't mind if we hike along with you, or did you want to go by yourselves?" Nick looked pensive.

Grace's eyes scanned her friends, her mouth agape. She was thankful Rebecca spoke up.

"We'd love some company." Rebecca smiled and broke the tension. The guys introduced themselves. Each was a fireman, EMT, or police officer.

"We're in good hands," Grace's eyes drifted to Nick and she smiled. "I think some of them are Boy Scouts, too."

That brought some good-natured laughter and the guys hustled to store their beer and food inside the cabin. Grace laced up her well-worn hiking boots and grabbed her stainless-steel bottle and filled it with water. She tucked a few granola bars into her vest. Her hair was piled on top of her head and wrapped with an old faded bandana. She could imagine what she looked like in the plaid flannel shirt and fleece vest. Her knobby knees were revealed even though she wore long shorts to hide them. Of course, she'd left her make-up at home. All she had was raspberry Chapstick and bug repellant.

The guys all hiked wearing sneakers and brought a beer bong with them. Grace walked with Sarah and Rebecca and noticed Ingrid had taken great interest in Nick right away. Every so often, Grace noticed he glanced back toward her and smiled a little. It was as if he was keeping an eye on her, looking out for her, or at least that's how she felt.

As the autumn leaves and twigs crunched beneath their feet, Grace captured a few photographs with her phone. Ingrid was glued to Nick, or so it appeared. They paused at one vista that overlooked the campsite where they were staying. Nick's friends were chatting and joking around with one another. Their mood was lighthearted, happy. Paul, the guy getting married was tall, dark and handsome and smiled a lot. As everyone sat on an outcropping of rocks to enjoy the view, Nick appeared next to Grace.

"This is beautiful, the scenery, I mean."

He seemed bashful and different out of uniform, but she liked that about him.

"Yes, I love this time of year. It's my favorite – sort of the last fling of summer."

Nick leaned close to her ear, "Your friend there is quite a chatterbox. Nothing like you."

Grace smiled and glanced toward Ingrid. "She's a lot of fun."

"But, not like *you*." He whispered. "I don't want to step out of line, but are you seeing someone right now?"

Grace hesitated. "No."

"Just finished something?"

"Sort of."

"Hmm. You're making this difficult, Gracie."

She gazed into his eyes filled with mischief. "I'm not trying to…"

The others called to them and they continued the trek up the mountain trail until they came to the summit. By then, Grace and Nick had hiked side by side for almost two hours. She slid a honey-oat granola bar out of her vest.

"Want one?"

"How'd you know I was starving?" Nick smiled and took the bar from her fingers. His hand brushed hers and he held it, like he did in the ER the first time she met him. Maybe it was his reaction to receiving food, but she loved it – his hand holding hers.

"I'm enjoying the view, but you know I'm not talking about the foliage." Nick spoke softly. His eyes seemed to be drinking in every detail about her.

Grace blushed and turned away. "I can only imagine what I look like today. I so did not dress for company."

"What do you mean? Damn it, girl, you're stunning. I can't believe some guy hasn't gotten you wrapped up."

Grace was not accustomed to being showered with compliments. With Michael, it had been much different. He was nice at first, but later, he was demanding. She had promised herself she'd never fall for that routine again, yet here she was putting herself next to a guy who could crush her spirit if she let him in.

"No. There's no one."

"Then, I've gotta ask you a question." She watched as Nick inhaled deeply. "Would a guy like me even have a *chance* with a chick like you?"

Grace suddenly realized how nervous and insecure Nick was. But, more importantly, it dawned on her that he had no clue how smitten she already was with him.

"Yeah, you've got a chance, Boy Scout."

She watched a smile take over his face, the look of relief. He leaned closer and Grace felt his lips touching hers, tentatively at first. His tongue swept over the seam of her lips briefly and when he stood to help her up, he whispered, "Damn, that's raspberry. My favorite." His big hand covered hers and the Nordic blue of his eyes melted her as she rose before him. She was more than enthralled and the rest of the hike she felt as if his eyes were undressing her. Instead of shutting down, she flirted with him and giggled at the funny comments he made with his friends.

Back at the campsite she watched him build and stoke the fire. When Nick sat next to her in a double Adirondack chair, he took her hand in his and pulled her body closer. She felt his strong arm move around her shoulders, and it sort of hung there as he leaned back and kept a running repertoire with his friends. She studied his face unhurriedly, feature by feature. His profile was handsome, his brow prominent, his face youthful, but his eyes held something deeper. He engaged in conversation with the others, but his gaze seemed to hold a private message for her.

Everyone was hungry and her girlfriends helped unpack the food to be grilled. The meal was thrown together in a communal fashion. The girls brought chicken, the guys brought beef – with special rubs and sauces – and plenty of potato salad. As Grace stood to help out, Nick gently pulled her back toward him.

"I'm doing the cooking tonight for you. You're on vacation this weekend, Gracie."

"Oh, you don't have to…." Grace couldn't get the words out. She watched as he speared the meat and cooked it perfectly. Every so often, he turned to glance her way. Grace busied herself putting beer into the cooler. Ingrid and Sarah stood next to her.

"Damn. He's a keeper!" Ingrid gushed.

"Yeah, where'd you meet him?" Sarah queried.

"In the ER. He's a cop. I know all of them." Grace tried to sound casual. She didn't want to let on that she was already nurturing a crush on Nick Kozlovsky.

Her girlfriends disappeared as Nick came toward her with two plates.

"Dinner is served." Nick's smile was intoxicating. Grace sipped a beer and picked at her food, unable to think of anything except kissing him again.

"Not hungry?" Nick's eyes were on her.

"Yes. I'm just a lot slower than you." She took another bite. The food was delicious, but her stomach had butterflies again.

Nick speared a chunk of potato salad and brought it to her lips. She took it in as she felt his lingering stare. "Mmm."

"Is it good?" He asked. "Be honest."

"It's delicious!"

"Good. I made it." Nick seemed proud.

One of the guys had a guitar and the girls were singing along with him. Grace felt Nick's hand pull her up.

"Want to go for a little walk?" He asked.

"Sure. I need to use the rest room." Grace figured she was killing his interest with that comment, but he led her to her cabin.

"I'll wait outside, if you want." Nick offered.

"You can come in." Grace eyed him from the stairs.

The two slipped inside the dark, solace of the cabin. Nick lit the gas sconce on the wall and waited by the doorway. In the bathroom, Grace used a Coleman lantern on a shelf to illuminate her face. Oh God, she was a mess. She removed the bandana and brushed her hair. Then ran the water and washed her face and brushed her teeth. Raspberry Chapstick. She rummaged through her backpack, not even a breath mint.

"You okay in there?" Nick yelled.

"Yes, I'll be right out." Grace turned off the Coleman lantern. This was as good as it was going to get. She took a deep breath and let it out slowly.

She didn't know why, but she wanted Nick to gawk at her some more. She'd missed the feeling of being the center of attention for a man, especially one that looked like Nick. Oh yes, she was feeling the physical pull of attraction a little stronger every time she felt his touch or heard his voice.

In the back of her mind, she could hear her therapist, be careful with your heart. Don't just give it away to anyone. It's too important. Vet them. Use your head. Take things slow. Get to know the guy.

* * *

Nick had been standing in the corner of the cabin listening to water running off and on for fifteen minutes. He sensed Grace was a bit nervous or maybe she didn't feel well. The moment she stepped into the room, his eyes traveled over her and he noticed she'd been freshening up. Of course, she was a woman. Damn, she was an incredible beauty today in the bright sunlight, but right now she was even more gorgeous, if that was even possible. The gaslight highlighted her ivory skin surrounded by thick chocolate-colored hair. Her pale blue eyes, fringed with dark lashes, met his and he felt his hormones go into overdrive.

He stepped forward and instinctively wrapped his arms around her. Her face turned upward and he grazed her lips with his. The velvet softness of her mouth sampled earlier on the hike remained in the forefront of his mind. He'd been waiting to kiss her again. His lips melded with hers and everything about Grace, was soft, smooth and feminine. His tongue probed and he tasted the distinct flavor of raspberry. He felt her smile as he kissed her, but he could tell she liked whatever he was doing. *Good, she wanted him.* His arms enclosed her snugly and he allowed one hand to move to the small of her back. He felt her uneven breath against his cheek as he held her. He suddenly realized he hadn't lovingly kissed a woman like this since he could remember, probably since junior high. For some reason, it was always the women who overpowered him.

Grace's eyelashes fluttered against his cheek, and he couldn't stop himself from uttering the words, "I want you."

Her chin dropped against his chest with a sigh of pleasure.

His hand explored the hollow of her back as he moved his mouth over hers, devouring the supple feel of her full lips. He'd never wanted a woman as much as he wanted Grace right then.

The door to the cabin burst open and Nick stepped away from Grace as his head turned toward the sound of her giggling girlfriends.

"Oh sorry!" Ingrid squealed. Sarah and Rebecca were close behind.

"That's okay." Grace tittered nervously.

Nick felt Grace remove her hand from his chest as she spoke. Then she patted his arm. "I was just examining Nick's injuries. He's healing well. There's not a lot of light in here."

Nick took his chance to leave.

"Hey, you girls have a good night. See you on the river bright and early in the morning for some crazy fun. Stay safe."

Nick moved toward the doorway as the girls stepped inside. He felt their eyes on him and they fell silent as he moved past them to the doorway.

He never felt so embarrassed in his life. Even though he knew they couldn't see how excited he'd become, when he got outside he adjusted his jeans to accommodate his growing interest in Grace. He didn't just *want* Grace; he couldn't stop *thinking* about wanting her. This was going to be a night filled with distractions, or so he hoped.

The guys all teased him when he entered the cabin.

"Where ya been, lover?"

"She's cute, can't blame you."

One of them tossed Nick a sparkling water, Raspberry flavored. "How'd you know that was my favorite flavor?"

Fake yawns abounded and the guys were pretending they were exhausted. Good, the prank they were going to play on Paul required him to be sleeping and Paul had just enough beer for that. Nick stepped into the rustic bathroom of his cabin and sent a text to Grace, thankful he'd gotten her cell number the night he was in the hospital. *Sorry for the interruption – I can't stop thinking of you.*

He rummaged through a bag from the pharmacy and found the red fingernail polish and some other stuff. His phone vibrated with a response from Grace. *How'd you get my number?*

He smiled. *It was on the card you handed to me in the hospital. You secretly wanted me to call you, I just know you did.* He added a smiley face.

Grace messaged back. *See you tomorrow on the river, my blue knight.*

For a second he stood there in the darkness absorbing her message. He was her knight, or so he hoped. He smiled at the thought. He wished he was alone in a cabin with Grace and all this bachelor party stuff had melted away. No longer could he focus on pranks or colorful stories with his friends. He wanted *her.* He knew the rest of the night he'd suffer from this temporary madness. He was breathless to see her tomorrow, hold her hand, gaze into her eyes. He had lots of experience with women, but never had a kiss affected him as the one he shared earlier with Grace. Now that he thought about it, he rarely kissed the other women. It was usually a hormonal surge, followed by a rush of primal instinct. With Grace, everything was completely different ~ soft and sexy, sweet and beautiful.

Tom poked his head around the corner, breaking the trance.

"You coming, Romeo?"

Nick padded barefoot into the room where Paul was softly snoring. The other guys were still awake, waiting for him to do the unthinkable. Nick painted Paul's toenails a bright red with the nail polish. The hardest part was not making any noise, and stifling his overwhelming urge to chuckle. He worked with great precision. Paul stirred once or twice but remained asleep. One of the other guys streaked his black hair with frosted highlights. The stuff smelled awful. Oh God, he looked like a skunk when they finished. They whispered about shaving his eyebrows off, but decided against it. His bride-to-be would kill them. As they suppressed laughter, they took photos of him sleeping. Finally, Nick turned off the gaslight. He hadn't done this stuff since the last fishing trip they'd taken together. He was the one who got painted up that time.

Exhausted, he slid into his bunk, took a deep breath and exhaled. As he closed his eyes, he replayed the moment with Grace and kissing her. She was so different than Kristie or Beth or any of the others. This wasn't going to be easy. He'd have to work for this one. But he was willing to do whatever it would take to win her. At some point, he hoped she would be open to talking about her past. There had to be other guys, plural. There was no way a woman like that could be single without having had *some* experience.

And, at some point, he'd have to talk about his past, too. That was the difficult bit for him. Whenever any potential love interest asked him questions about his life growing up, he'd cleverly avoided answering their questions. Making jokes about his upbringing, he'd say things like--- I was raised by wolves...or, I was born in a cabbage patch. Most of the women he'd been with didn't really push him for details. They'd just laugh when he said those things. They were interested in other qualities. And, that was fine with him. But, this was different. The shame, the sadness, and humiliation about his past life, if revealed, couldn't be rescinded. And, he had no idea what Grace would think about him after that. He just hoped she'd still view him as her knight. But there was no way to know what her reaction might be.

* * *

Grace tossed and turned in her bunk all night. That kiss from Nick was unexpected. Once again, she reminded herself to go slowly. Her heart wasn't healed from the last experience. At least that's what the therapist had told her. But Nick was *different* than Michael and every other guy she'd met. There was no doubt about the physical attraction, but this went far beyond that already. She hardly knew Nick, but there was this *thing* about him. Grace felt like she was a ship adrift in a harbor and he was a safe mooring. Steady. Calm. Knowledgeable. Patient. These were all the qualities she'd dreamt about in a man and now he was sleeping in the cabin next to hers.

By sunrise, the girls were in their wetsuits and ready to go white water rafting. Grace was the last one to rise and they were complaining that she was taking too long.

"Come on, Grace! You're usually the first one up. Why so slow this morning?" Ingrid seemed to be the most impatient.

"I'm coming. I just want to brush my teeth and comb my hair." Grace yelled from the bathroom.

"This ain't no beauty contest." Sarah uttered.

"She kissed that guy last night. The cute cop... What's his name?" Ingrid was starting something Grace didn't want to finish.

"Nick something. I couldn't pronounce his last name." Rebecca laughed.

Grace finally emerged in her wetsuit with a few items strapped to her body, like her waterproof Go-Pro camera, and goggles.

"Come on, nerd girl, they're waiting!" Ingrid tugged her outside.

Nick and the guys were lingering outside their cabin and Grace felt his eyes on her the moment she stepped out. The water shoes made her walk funny. She sensed the guys were laughing at her, but then realized it wasn't her they were joking about. *Poor Paul.* His hair was striped black and white, perfect for Halloween.

The group scrambled toward the river's edge and each got into a raft. The guides ran through a safety checklist. Grace was nervous. What if she had to go to the bathroom? What if she fell out of the raft as it shot the rapids? A myriad of scenes flashed through her mind as she glanced toward Nick. He seemed to be ignoring the guide and was looking at her. When he winked, she smiled nervously and turned away. Sheer terror gripped her as she climbed into the raft with her best friends, as she murmured a silent prayer. *How the hell did she get talked into this?* She couldn't remember. It was over beer and pizza.

At first the river seemed calm and smooth. It was a bright sunny autumn day. The raft drifted along and she paddled in unison with the other girls to stay toward the middle of the river. Early morning sunlight filtered through the trees and she watched a horde of wasps being born right before her eyes. They drifted on an air current above them, tiny legs dangling. That's what she felt like ~ a helpless tiny creature at the mercy of the river current.

Without warning, the turbulence of the river increased dramatically and the first change in topography was surprising, even though the guide described it perfectly. Grace felt a moment of uncontrollable panic. The raft picked up speed and the paddle was used now for steerage. Rocks loomed ahead and she took a deep breath and counted to four. Her heart was racing and not in a way that felt good. She caught a glimpse of Nick and the guys in their raft. They were laughing and swearing up a storm. Soon their voices were eclipsed by the deafening sound of the approaching rapids, the first tier. The guide was saying something but she couldn't hear it. Grace had her Go-Pro camera filming since boarding the raft. She only hoped it didn't film her ultimate demise. What a horrible thought ~ she could imagine the headline: *young woman killed in white water rafting trip and her camera filmed it all. Watch this on YouTube!*

Shooting the rapids was beyond terrifying. Good thing she didn't have time to think about it. The girls were tossed into the raft by the rushing water as they attempted to avoid the rocks. They fell atop one another and as they sat up the raft lurched wildly in the opposite direction. Luckily the river was high and the rocks didn't protrude as much, but when they hit the smooth rocks the raft would bounce off and Grace held on for dear life. The girls were tossed around like rag dolls. Several of them lost their grip and fell *into* the raft, luckily.

No so for the guys. One of them fell out of the raft and the guide tossed a line to him. Grace watched in awe as he pulled himself back in with the help of the others. Nick had pinned the raft with the paddle and Paul had done the same. Their quick reaction and teamwork saved their friend from drowning. The women were ahead of them now, moving rapidly down the second tier, then the long chute -- and Grace could see the pool of water below. It appeared to be calm, but she wasn't. Swirling whirlpools formed that could suck you under if you fell in. Well, at least that's what Ingrid told her. Grace felt as if her heart was beating right out of her chest.

For a long while they paddled in the lower basin where the current was more controlled. Grace enjoyed this part the most. The scary stuff was over. She saw a bald eagle swoop at the river's edge to catch a meal. She spotted a doe and a fawn lingering in the tall grass. Every time she glanced Nick's way, he was eyeing her.

She had no idea how much time had elapsed, but it had been hours. At the very end of the ride, the rafts met and nearly collided. She watched an eddy form in the slowly moving water of the basin. *They'd made it.* The girls were screaming and fist-bumping. The guys were swearing and high-fiving. At one point, Nick caught her attention, winked at her and gave her a thumbs-up. Grace felt exhilaration race through her. She'd survived. For a second, as she observed Nick laughing, she realized this was how he felt every day on his job. He cheated death and lived another day. Each one of the men had highly dangerous professions, yet they were content to have this moment, this hour, this day. Their smiles weren't just happy – they were ecstatic. They lived in the moment, something she wished she could do.

For a little while, after pulling the rafts out of the water, everyone had to use the restroom which was a portable one, not Grace's favorite, but it didn't matter. Thank goodness, the wetsuit had a flap for just that purpose. When she emerged, Nick was standing outside nearby as if waiting for her.

"How was it?"

"The portable bathroom or the raft ride?" Grace giggled.

"The raft ride. You didn't get too many bumps and bruises, did you?"

Grace noticed his furrowed brow, those pale blue eyes gazing ardently into hers. He was genuinely concerned.

"I fell in the raft a few times, and did a lot of screaming, but I'm fine."

"I heard you screaming." Nick moved closer. "I thought you might've been hurt."

Grace felt like an idiot. She had probably let out an ear-piercing shriek more than once. But she couldn't seem to keep it inside. She had been filled with adrenaline at the moment. Now she felt completely relaxed, almost tired.

"Wow! That was some ride." She smiled.

"Yeah, I loved it." Nick moved closer, "I want to get out of this wetsuit."

"What happened to Paul's hair?"

"Oh, we had a little fun last night. He's getting married in ten days. Hey, you want to go to the wedding with me. I have an invitation, plus one -- and I don't have a plus one." Nick let the words tumble out and Grace was taken by surprise.

"Let me check my work schedule. But, yes, if I'm free." Grace answered.

"Hey, we're starving. You guys coming?" Ingrid walked behind Grace.

"Yes, coming." Grace ran to catch up with her.

Back at the cabin, Grace got into the shower and hot water never felt so wonderful. She washed her hair and toweled dry, all the while thinking of Nick and what the night would be like. He had officially asked her out. He was interested. She knew that from the first moment she'd laid eyes on him, he could be fun and exciting or a whole lot of trouble. She wasn't sure which yet.

It was 4 PM by the time the bonfire was built and the beer and food was strewn on the tops of the picnic tables. One of the guys was doing a slow cook barbeque and the aroma wafted through the air. Grace felt the hunger pangs in her stomach. The moment Nick noticed her, Grace felt his arm pulling her toward him.

"You are lovely tonight." He murmured and Grace turned away as she felt her face flush. Every time he touched her, he sent shockwaves of pleasure through her body all meeting in the same place, just below her naval. She hoped he didn't notice, but Grace had the distinct feeling that Nick had the ability to read her thoughts. Of course, he was a police officer, trained in human behavior. She imagined he could see right through her.

"Try some of this barbeque, this is Tom's special recipe. He started slow-cooking it last night." Nick lifted a fork to her mouth and she automatically parted her lips. Her eyes locked with his as she took the deliciously flavored meat into her mouth. Nick waited with child-like anticipation.

"What do you think?" He asked.

"Mmm. I love it."

Nick proceeded to put a plateful of food together for her, then brought it to the corner of the picnic table away from the crowd. While eating and talking together, Grace noticed how the firelight played off Nick's attractive face. He had an appealing boyish grin and his hair was askew. He seemed to be comfortable with himself. When he wasn't paying attention, her eyes drifted to the T-shirt beneath the unzipped fleece jacket and his chest. She watched as Nick got up from the picnic table and noticed how his worn Wrangler jeans fit his muscled rear. He had nearly perfect anatomy, rugged well-defined musculature on a six-foot frame.

"I forgot to ask," Nick was back again, "Did you want a beer?"

"Sure." Grace smiled. She watched him retrieve a cold one from the cooler and he got a cup. The cold beer tasted good with the barbeque. Nick had made the salad, which was a chopped concoction of a myriad of vegetables drizzled with his secret dressing. *Nothing was more delightful than a guy who could cook.*

"You're not having a beer?" She looked up at him.

"No. I don't do alcohol." Nick said matter-of-factly.

"Never?"

"I don't like the feeling of being out of control." Nick appeared somber when he spoke those words.

The others were drinking plenty of beer and staring skyward. They'd yell when they saw a shooting star. One of the guys was strumming a guitar. Grace had a second beer and listened to Nick's voice as he told her about each of his friends. When he smiled, he looked so young. He was only two years younger than she, but the way he carried himself, the way he spoke, gave her the impression he was much older than his years.

"Let's go for a walk." Nick took her hand and drew her toward him. Grace felt herself melting when he touched her. His warm broad hand held hers as they walked toward the river. Grace watched as he stepped up onto the porch of cabin 12, which was vacant. When the door opened, Grace was at the bottom of the stairs.

"How'd that happen?" She giggled.

"It's open… come on." Nick gestured to her.

As she stepped inside, he pushed the door closed and lit the gaslight with a match. Outside the raucous sound of laughter and echo of song filled the night air. Nick stood in front of her and cupped her face in his hands. As he captured her eyes with his, her pulse pounded. She was powerless and felt a ripple of excitement as his mouth came down upon hers. She could feel his heart beating against her own.

"Grace, you feel so… good."

She tingled as he uttered her name. His closeness was like a drug, lulling her to euphoria.

She was shocked by her own eager response to his lips and drank in the sweetness of his kiss.

"Raspberry Chapstick." He murmured. "I want to eat you up."

His hands unbuttoned her flannel shirt and he swept her long hair aside. Grace felt his thumb brush her erect nipple and listened to his breathing quicken. His lips were on her neck, his hand caressed her breast. He gazed into her eyes and moved his mouth to the pink bud; her hand automatically drew him there, her fingers in his hair. The touch of his lips on her breast caused a shiver of delight.

She unbuttoned his shirt and put her cheek against his chest and listened to his heart beat. She had wanted to do this from the first moment she saw him. He moved her onto the bed and looked into her eyes as he traced his fingertip across her lip. Her mouth took his finger in briefly and he tossed his shirt onto the floor.

"Damn, you're beautiful."

Filled with anticipation, Grace wanted him, all of him. His tongue tantalized her nipples, then his mouth covered hers and she felt his body atop her. He was erect, straining against those jeans. She reached down, unbuttoned, and heard him inhale sharply as she grabbed him. His hand roamed between her thighs and she moved her legs apart and whispered.

"Don't stop."

His hand slipped between her legs and she responded with a quivering urgency. She moved beneath him as he expertly caressed her warm moist center with his finger. *Oh, he knew what he was doing.* Passion pounded through her heart, her chest, her head, and she lost control. It was such a beautiful feeling. His skilled hand brought her to a breathless peak of delight. Waves of pleasure engulfed her. His mouth was on hers, his tongue probing the seam of her lips. She let him in. His hand moved his erection to the warm wet place between her thighs and as he moved between her legs, his breathing increased. His hardness electrified her as his hands slipped beneath her bottom. Penetration was slow, pleasurable, primal. Grace was swept away. Every nerve-ending fired simultaneously as she felt his release.

Moments later, she curled up within his solid core, he'd pulled a blanket over them. He smelled like soap and leather, and she inhaled the scent wanting to remember it. Her back was to him, and he brushed her hair aside and kissed that place below her ear. How did he know that was the special erogenous zone? She expected him to say something like, *was it good for you?* But this wasn't Michael, or any of the other guys who ended up being a two-month fling. No. *Nick was different.*

"Grace, that was…beautiful."

"Mmm." Was her response. She did not elaborate. She felt Nick's hand take hers and he entwined her fingers with his. The warmth of his hand and the way he nestled against her made her feel sheltered from the rest of the world. Grace didn't want him to see the single tear that slid down her cheek. As she closed her eyes, she exhaled. It was obvious to her that Nick enjoyed the afterglow as much as he did the main feature.

She had never experienced this before and was surprised by her own reaction, frightened really. She knew he had no idea he had moved her to tears. Nick fed something deep inside of her, a need, a want, a longing to be loved ~ not in a casual way, but loved in the way she'd read about in fairy tales. No one had made her feel this way and she didn't know what to do or say. He was an amazing human being, kind, loving, true blue ~ the guy she'd always dreamed of.

Chapter 8

Following Labor Day, Nick returned to the real world as he handcuffed a felon with outstanding warrants in his sector on a cool September evening. He went through his night shift with conflicting thoughts vying for his attention. He couldn't stop thinking of Grace. Her name described her perfectly. She was grace and beauty and everything he'd dreamt of in a woman. Even dressed as a tomboy with no make-up, she was feminine and downright gorgeous. But, another female was ever present in his mind – his sister, Sophia. At roll call, he asked his superiors if they'd get eyes out for her. It wasn't a formal BOLO, but her description was given and Nick would be notified if anyone came upon her.

The radio jolted him out of his momentary contemplation.

"Unit 12 – car accident on Main and Compton. Ambulance on the way. Unit 19 – please respond as back-up…" Nick listened to the urgent tone of the dispatcher's voice.

Nick immediately answered. "Unit 12 responding."

With lights and siren blaring, he raced to the scene. At first glance, it looked bad. A large box truck had crushed a Nissan compact, mangled it really. The car was now a mass of twisted metal as gasoline pooled on the ground; the occupants were not moving. The truck driver was staggering around in a daze.

"I didn't see them…."

He had taken a hit against the steering wheel, Nick surmised. He helped the man sit down on the curb. He had a gash on his forehead where he hit the steering wheel, but didn't seem to be hurt badly.

"Help is on the way…" Nick quickly flashed a beam into his face. His pupils responded normally. "I've got to check the others."

As he moved the flashlight over the two bodies trapped in the Nissan, he noticed one had blonde hair. Neither occupant was moving. A small purse was strewn among the wreckage. He grabbed it and touched the young woman's hand.

"Ma'am, can you speak?"

No response. He moved to the other occupant who had gone through the windshield in the passenger seat. She had short dark hair. Her neck was broken, head twisted, and blood soaked her face beyond recognition. The sound of the ambulance and the jaws-of-life were behind him. He opened the purse and pulled out a driver's license with the name of Sophia Anderson on it. As he did, his heart felt as if it momentarily stopped.

"Damn, that's my sister!" Nick yelled to Officer Johnson who was next to him.

Nick felt Johnson's big hands on both of his shoulders, pulling him away.

Johnson forced Nick to look into his eyes as he spoke.

"Hey. Let me do my thing. You've got to stand-by, Nick. I'll do everything I can for her, man."

"I can't just stand-by. That's my *sister*. I need to help." Nick tried to rein in his emotions, but he felt himself careening out of control. He watched helplessly as the extraction unit did its work, but it didn't look hopeful. Sophia's limp body was gently turned over and Johnson and the ambulance team worked diligently examining her, trying to revive her. They went above and beyond what any typical rescue team would, and Nick felt his heart breaking. She was only 19. He wanted to know what happened, yet in the recess of his mind he *didn't* want to know. He wanted to remember Sophia, as the brazen, untamed, beauty that she was. She was a spitfire, wild and free, just like his mom.

With tear-filled eyes, he rummaged through her purse and found heroin, needles, and money -- lots of money. He knew, as a police officer, he'd have to turn the purse in and he felt Officer Johnson's hand on his shoulder.

"I'm sorry, Nick. She was killed instantly, upon impact."

Nick handed the purse to Johnson.

"Please give me her belongings, once the investigation is finished." Nick mumbled as he closed his eyes.

"Yes. Of course. I'll tag everything and make note of it. Why don't you go back to the station? I'll finish your shift. I'm sorry, man. This is horrible. I mean, it's bad enough to scoop up complete strangers, but when it's your own – I'm really sorry, man. I'm here if you need me." Officer Johnson put his arm around Nick for a moment.

Officer Herrick was next to him. "Hey, Nick – I'm sorry about this. It's a damned shame. You need to go home. Get a night's sleep. We've got this. You need to take some time. I just called the boss. He said you're off shift for a few days." Herrick touched his shoulder gently as Nick felt his head fall to his chest, defeated.

Feeling numb, Nick nodded and climbed into his cruiser. He drove to the police station and parked in the lot, sitting there for a few minutes in the dark as he tried to absorb what just happened. He dropped his face into his hands and sobbed. *Why?* Why did it have to be her? Why was it *heroin*? Sophia was still young, beautiful, her whole life ahead of her.

After he pulled himself together, he walked inside. He made arrangements to have his sister's body under his care for burial arrangements. When Nick told the desk sergeant he was next-of-kin, Sergeant Adams was polite and kind, and said all the right things. But Nick couldn't seem to think straight. It felt like he was in a slow-motion nightmare and he wanted to awaken, but couldn't.

He knew what he had to do. He'd walked so many other citizens through this same process, he was all too familiar with what would come next.

The first call he made was to his aunt, Brenda. His heart broke as he heard her weeping on the phone. Katie and Julia took the phone away from her. He knew they'd take the news hard. They were young and looked up to Sophia. His next call was to Natalie, now 21, living out of state attending college. She, too, wept uncontrollably. She was close to Sophia growing up and hesitated when she left Cherryfield, but Nick had coaxed her to go and find her dream. He'd promised to watch over Sophia. He hated himself for not fulfilling that pledge. His younger twin brothers, Victor and Alexander, now 24, always had each other to lean on. Each phone call was difficult and he couldn't regain his composure afterward.

Exhausted, Nick drove home. But for some reason he swept through Grace's neighborhood. Being in her presence, even for a short while, would somehow comfort him. Tonight, she was off and her Land Rover was parked at the tiny house, but another vehicle was there, too. He paused at the end of her driveway and jotted down the license plate of the Jaguar on a piece of paper. Maybe a family member was visiting Grace. He'd called her three times since the night at the cabin, but she texted him back cheery messages as if nothing happened between them. She managed to dodge his requests to see her. Nick was beginning to wonder if that was just another throw down for her. Maybe she wasn't the gracious angel he had imagined after all. He pushed that thought out of his mind for the moment. Grace had a life. She was a busy doctor. He wanted to think she wasn't avoiding him.

On the trek back to his apartment, he stopped in his Jeep to check on Paco. The injured vet was beginning to be an inspiration for him, even though he had imagined it to be the other way around. Paco came to the door immediately.

"Hey Nick. Come in…."

Nick sat on Paco's couch. As Paco reached to turn on the light, Nick whispered.

"Please, don't. I parked out back. No one knows I'm here. I'm messed up, Paco."

"What's going on?"

"My sister. She's dead. I found her. It was a car accident, but I found heroin in her purse."

Nick couldn't continue. He felt his throat constrict and fought the tears.

"Damn it, Paco, I was supposed to be her guardian. I'm the one who was supposed to protect her. I had no idea what the hell she was doing."

Diesel hopped up on the sofa and Nick felt the dog lean against him.

"He wants you to pet him." Paco said softly.

Nick's hand ran over Diesel's soft fur and the dog nudged him with his nose. Diesel rolled over and exposed his belly to Nick. His hand rubbed the canine's chest, and felt his heart beat. *Life. It was so fragile.* For a split second, he stopped thinking of his own angst and realized he knew nothing about Paco and what he'd been through.

Paco handed him a cold glass of water.

"She's in heaven, man. She's the lucky one."

An hour passed as Nick listened to Paco, who wasn't usually a talkative guy. Nick noticed he was a man of few words, but carefully chose the words he used. Paco interjected his own thoughts throughout the conversation but Nick realized he had done most of the talking. But, as Nick sat in the darkness of his small dwelling, he knew there was so much more to Paco than he'd originally thought.

Nick had suspected all along that Paco was still fighting his own internal war. Four tours in Afghanistan was only the beginning of it. His wife had left him while he was overseas. She'd spent all his money and ran off with another guy. He had been raising her child from another marriage and now he couldn't even see the little boy who had called him daddy.

"The worst part of my return home was the fact that I had to leave my canine behind. We were a team, Paco and Bam-Bam. Incendiary sniffing dogs were a huge part of this war. I ate, slept, and trained with Bam-Bam for five years. I trained him as a pup. Then, when it was time to come home, I wasn't allowed to take my dog. Coming home was not a happy occasion for me. The injuries to my spine from sniper bullets hobbled me. I have no feeling in my hands and feet most of the time. The nerve damage is extensive. But, I never wanted anyone's pity. I just wanted my dog. The sons-of-bitches wouldn't let me have him. He's dead. A friend of mine who left a couple of months later told me the locals killed all the dogs when we left the base in Afghanistan."

While in service, Paco had followed a strict regime every day. As Paco put it, "Eat, drink, work, sleep - rinse and repeat." He laughed about it, but he also gave Nick insight into living on the street. Paco had a routine, he moved forward every day with a sense of purpose.

"I had nothing until I met you last month. You've made a huge difference in my life, man. I'll help you in any way that I can. Your sister loved you, Nick. She had to. You're a great guy. You stepped in when there was no father figure. You did your best. This world is an ugly place. Many people get taken to the dark side. I've been there, man. Few people ever get out. Shit, I'm not telling you anything you don't already know. You're cleaning up the leftovers of society every day out there. Seeing people at their worst. Some crazy ass guy by the name of Nietzsche said, *that which you gaze upon, you become.* But not you. You're true blue, man. You forge ahead. I admire you. You're like some sort of Viking, wearing bulletproof armor, keeping your feelings inside. But, I know you have a heart and a soul. And, I'm damned sorry about your sister."

Nick was surprised when he stood to leave, Paco embraced him. There were no words, just an embrace that spoke volumes.

That night Nick had no trouble falling asleep. He'd left Paco's at midnight. He didn't bother to shower. He dropped into the unmade bed and slowly drifted into a dream state. In his own grief and sorrow, he thought about the details Paco had shared with him tonight. Lots of people would think that Bam-Bam was just a dog, but Nick understood Paco's suffering. To know his closest pal couldn't come home with him and to know how he met his demise must've been devastating. Not to mention how he suffered with the physical wounds of war. Yet, Paco seemed to understand Nick's loss on a deeper level.

Nick's last thought was rubbing Diesel's ears and how the dog gazed into his eyes with a knowing look. Diesel comforted him, sensed his pain. How could an animal be so perceptive? How could some human beings be so cold and indifferent? It would've cost nothing compared to other wasteful governmental spending, to bring the service dogs home with their handlers. The loss tore a hole in Paco's soul. He was healing, but it was a slow and painful process.

For the first time Nick realized that Paco was grieving the loss of so many things. Nick had been depressed before, but nothing compared to the black hole of despair he felt as he blamed himself for Sophia's loss. But when he imagined the black hole Paco was fighting to crawl out of, it gave him pause. Afghanistan, loss of his brothers, his canine, his health, his family.

As Nick's eyes closed, he contemplated his personal wars. The Bermuda Triangle. The unending procession of drug dealers, prostitution, addicts. Despair. Depression. Both men were engaged in a struggle. He had always thought of Paco as having a physical disability, with his broken back and addiction to methadone. But now he recognized that wasn't the case. It was as if Paco had held a mirror up to him. *For the first time, he realized that disabilities weren't physical, they were the fears harbored in the recesses of the human mind.*

* * *

Grace was shocked when she looked at her security camera and saw Michael Dean's face smiling back. His thick silvery hair and blue eyes looked the same, eager for her attention. She froze for a moment, remembering the words of her therapist. *This is not over, Grace. You need to be strong.* Although her heart skipped a beat when she saw it was him, she spoke to Michael through the speaker and asked him what he wanted. She imagined a red light in her head blinking *caution*.

"Grace. I need to talk with you."

His voice sent chills down her spine. She had forgotten how incredibly attractive he was. She had an overwhelming urge to open the door and pull him inside and ask him all about his life without her. It was her night off; how did he know she'd be home? She didn't care at that moment. She had dreamt about touching him, and in the dream, she'd experienced indescribable joy as he wrapped her in his arms, buried his face in her hair, whispered the words she so wanted to hear.

"Oh, Grace, I missed you so much, baby."

He now spoke the words into her security camera, standing on the stoop in front of her house, but they rang hollow. She remained inside, trembling, staring at his picture on the screen. She took a deep breath before responding. It had been eight months since she'd seen him. Her therapist would've been proud.

"I'm not letting you in, Michael, so you should leave." *There. It felt good to say it.* So good, she added, "Go home to your wife and family. I'm done with this."

Michael's face twisted. His smile vanished. He'd turned away from the camera and he appeared to be crying. His voice was halting when he spoke.

"I left Jeanine. We're going through a divorce, and it will be final in a few weeks. I live here in Connecticut now. I found a job in West Haven, it's a cardiology group. I have a home on Ocean Avenue, it's beautiful, Grace. You'd love it. It's a short drive from here."

Grace was in a state of shock, and remained motionless as she tried to focus on his words.

"Grace, listen to me. You blocked me on your phone, on Facebook, your e-mail. I had no other way to tell you this other than sending you a handwritten letter. And, if I had done that, I figured you would've ripped it up without reading it. I couldn't take that chance. I had to come here to talk with you to let you know I love you. My marriage is ending. Two of the kids are heading off to college and the other two, well – let's just say they all know about us. My wife told them everything."

The therapist hadn't told Grace what to do if *this* happened. It wasn't a scenario they'd played out in her sessions. The psychologist told Grace the odds would be *infinitesimal* for a man to leave his wife and four children for a mistress he'd bedded for more than four years. *But now she was faced with that one in a million chance.*

Stay strong, she heard the little voice in her head trying to boost her confidence. "Michael, I'm not ready for this. You've come out of the blue like a bolt of lightning. It's late at night. I need time to digest what you're saying."

"Will you at least unblock me on your cell phone? I think we need to talk." His request seemed reasonable enough at the moment.

"Okay. But, you have to leave right now. I can't talk with you. Please leave."

She watched as he slowly retreated and got into his Jaguar and drove away. He didn't seem angry, more like defeated. She exhaled. Her fingers shook as she dialed her therapist. Even though it was late at night, this wasn't the first time she'd done so.

"Doctor Child's answering service. Can I help you?"

"Yes, it's Grace Robertson. Can you have her call me? It's urgent."

"Yes. It may be a few minutes, but I will contact her."

Grace thanked the answering service and hung up. Her heart was beating wildly and she stared at her phone. Should she unblock Michael Dean? She told him she would, but she hesitated for a second, then decided to speak to her therapist first.

While glancing at her phone, a text arrived from Nick Kozlovsky. *My sister is dead.*

She messaged back, *Oh, I am so sorry to hear that Nick.*

But there was no reply back from Nick. She would stop by his apartment in the morning to see him. Her shift would begin at 3 PM. He was probably wondering why she hadn't responded to his invitations for coffee and lunch. He had no idea how difficult it was for her the night they made love, and she'd thought of nothing since. Nick filled her soul with warmth. He was a tender lover, so different than Michael in every way. But she wasn't sure she was ready to give her heart away again.

Her phone chimed and there was no caller ID. Grace answered and it was Doctor Childs. "What's going on, Grace? Talk to me." She was always straightforward and to the point.

"He's was here, on my doorstep. He wants to see me."

"Don't fall for the trap he is setting for you, Grace. We talked about the possibility of him telling you he would leave his wife. He told you he left, but he's not legally divorced. It's a ploy to get you back."

"But, he's moved out of the house. He bought a place on Ocean Avenue, he's working at a cardiology practice in West Haven. It's just a matter of time before the divorce will be final."

"You *want* him? After all he's put you through? Oh, Grace, you *need* to come and see me tomorrow. I'll make time for you at lunch. I'll order a sandwich for you."

"You're right. I'll be there at Noon."

Grace hung up the phone. She tapped Michael's phone number and unblocked him. He could now call, e-mail and text her. She figured she owed him that much, at the very least. She slept fitfully that night, with the thought of Michael showing up on her doorstep. In her dream, she had opened the door and thrown her arms around him, inhaling the aroma of his cologne mingled with the smell that was Michael. Fifteen years older than her, he was handsome, dignified, sexy – and was one of those guys who caused women's heads to swivel when he walked by. As a professor, many of the female students had a crush on him. *But, he'd chosen her.*

Chapter 9

Nick woke later than usual with the task of arranging his sister's funeral service before him. When he glanced at his phone, he noticed Grace had at least acknowledged his text regarding the death of his sister. As he made a pot of coffee, his phone rang.

"Where the hell have you been?" Kristie huffed. "You were supposed to do my brakes."

"My sister died. I've been making arrangements." Nick whispered.

"What? Oh shit. I'm sorry." Kristie moaned. "Which sister?"

"Sophia."

"What…happened?" Kristie asked.

"Auto accident. I was the first responder."

There was a long pause in the conversation.

"Hey. Listen, Kristie…bring your car up to Shane. I'll have him give you a discount on the brakes. I can't do it, babe, I'm sorry."

After she hung up, Nick called Shane. He told him about Sophia's death and asked if he'd do

Kristie's brake job. Shane was accommodating and filled with emotion on the phone.

Nick wanted more than ever to see Grace again. It had become more than a want; it was a strong need. She comforted him in a way that no other woman ever had. He took the chance and called her.

"Hello Nick." Her voice was warm and reassuring, feminine yet professional.

"Can I see you? I need to see you." *Damn. He sounded so desperate right now*. He imagined she was thinking he was beneath her, a loser. How could she get rid of him?

"Right now?" She asked.

"Yes. I'm taking a shower, but yes. Right now."

"I'll be there in 15 minutes." She hung up. Her response completely shocked him.

Nick scrambled into the shower and scrubbed from head to toe. He tore through his closet and found a clean pair of jeans and a flannel shirt. Hot damn. She was coming to *see* him. The soft knock on the door told him it was her. The other women always pounded on it. His pants were on, but his shirt was unbuttoned. When he opened the door, Grace stepped over the threshold and slid her arms around his waist. She laid her cheek upon his chest. Her face was cool against his skin, still warm from the shower.

"I'm sorry about Sophia. There are no words that can take your pain away." She murmured as she lingered in his embrace.

This was exactly what he needed. Her body against his, her breath on his chest. His hand caressing her long thick hair scented with sweetness. He did not want her to release him. It felt as if her heart beating next to his was some sort of tonic that he needed at that moment or he would die. Her touch nurtured him in an inexplicable way. Maybe it was because she was a doctor and she had the ability to heal. All he knew was no one had ever affected him as she did.

He spontaneously cupped her beautiful face in his hands, her tear-filled eyes met his. His lips brushed hers, but this kiss was different than the ones in the cabin. Grace kissed his lips, then his nose, chin, and cheek. Her hands moved behind him, and she clutched his back drawing herself even closer. Her lips moved to his ear, and Nick felt himself rising to the occasion. How he wanted her, not just now but forever.

Grace moved slightly.

"You okay?" He felt her eyes on the eagle tattoo as she began buttoning his shirt.

"Yeah. I'm just raw, you know?"

Grace tucked herself into a chair at his tiny kitchen table. Nick put a mug of coffee in front of her.

She tilted her head and gazed into his eyes.

"How can I help?"

"I need to arrange everything, *details*."

Nick's gaze was riveted to her face. He hadn't seen her since the rafting trip over a week ago. She was even more gorgeous than the photos he had on his iPhone. He drank in every detail while she spoke. Her hair was pulled back and he noticed the tiny earrings she'd worn the first time he saw her in the ER. Her eyes were kind, calm, and he felt as if she could see inside his mind, read his deepest thoughts. She sipped coffee and made notes on a pad of paper that had somehow appeared on his table.

For an hour, Grace walked through the tasks that needed to be completed. After talking with Nick about his family, she suggested cremation. Sophia's injuries were severe.

"How about having a small service at your Aunt Brenda's home? Your other siblings can travel there in a few days. Maybe get a platter of food from Lentini's. And, one other thing, Nick, you need to find some photos of Sophia, and get your sisters to compose a celebration of her life with them. Sophia was a lovely young woman. She died in a tragic accident. That's all they need to know."

Nick processed everything Grace was saying. As horrible as it seemed, he was mentally calculating everything in his mind. Cremation, paying travel fare for his siblings to come home, buying food. His savings account was on life support. But he didn't want Grace to know about his financial concerns. *This was embarrassing.* When she asked, he said he had enough money to take care of everything. He knew he'd need to get extended credit on his card, which was already to the max.

"You are a cop. I know what your salary is. And, I know you are supporting some of your siblings. It is admirable, what you are doing. You're a wonderful man, Nick. But, you put yourself last in the equation. I wish you'd let me help."

Her words touched him. How she knew all of that, he wasn't sure. He didn't remember saying those things. But people talked in Cherryfield. Everyone knew he'd come up the hard way. But no one ever made him see himself as Grace just did. All of what she said was true. How did she know him so well already?

"No, but thanks for the offer. I'll take care of this." He nodded.

He felt Grace's eyes studying him.

"How about Friday. That will give you enough time to talk with your family members." Grace rose and drifted toward the doorway. Nick didn't want her to leave just yet.

"Let's have lunch together." he moved close behind her. "I miss you, Grace. I can't stop thinking about Labor Day weekend."

"We'll talk about that later. You've got to get through *this* week, and I do, too."

He didn't know what she meant by the latter part of that sentence. Then, he remembered the Jaguar parked in her driveway last night.

"You had company last night."

"Yes. An old friend. I can't talk about it right now. I have a lunch appointment." She moved closer to the door and opened it.

Nick grasped her hand gently and kissed her upturned palm. Her eyes danced with his and she smiled.

"I'll answer your calls. I'm sorry, I've got to go for now."

The ancient wooden door creaked as it slowly closed. Nick stood there spellbound while he listened to Grace's footsteps in the hallway. Her vehicle started and she was gone. The sound of his stomach growling made him realize he hadn't eaten. As he finished dressing, he wondered who Grace was meeting for lunch.

Nick stopped at the drive-through for breakfast and pulled out the piece of paper with the license plate number written on it. When he arrived at the police station, he checked to see if his cruiser had been repaired. The back window had been replaced. He unlocked the door and slipped inside. Smelled good. Someone had cleaned it. He turned on the automatic license plate recognition and tapped the number into it. The name Michael Dean came up. It was a New York plate. Shit. This was the mystery guy on her Facebook page, the one she'd unfriended, or so he suspected. He wondered what the backstory was.

As he walked inside the building, his coworkers seized the chance to give him their personal condolences. He stopped in to see the detectives and one of them nodded to him and motioned toward the hallway.

Detective Wallingford leaned in and Nick stood close. "What's up?"

"Hey, the footage you gave us from your confidential informant is paying off." Wallingford whispered.

"Good. He said he'd have more information for you soon."

"Who is this guy – your informant – exactly how're you paying him? You know department policy and all of that." Nick knew Wallingford was looking out for him.

"I buy him groceries, that's it. He's not looking for a big payday. That's not his style."

Wallingford slipped Nick an envelope.

"I ran this by the chief and he approved it. Basically, I told him I had an informant. I don't want you putting your own money out for police work. Anonymous informants are critical in solving these cases. I'll drop this off once a week to you, keep the guy on the string, you know? Oh, and Nick, I'm sorry about your sister. All the more reason to catch these dealers. They're infiltrating our town and we've got to stop them."

"Yeah. I know."

He left the police building and headed for Paco's little dwelling at Strictly Storage. Inside, Paco was cooking quesadilla. Paco opened the door and Nick sat on the kitchen bar stool and laid the envelope on the counter.

"Your information is helping ~ keep it coming." Nick murmured.

"How're you holding up?" Paco's dark eyes examined him.

"I'm okay. Well, I'm not *really* okay. It's hard to believe I'll never see Sophia alive again – never be able to tell her how I felt. She had a difficult childhood, you know? I always wanted to shield her from the worst, but I didn't. I was too damned busy with my own life."

"It's not your fault, man." Paco spoke the words softly.

"I know. But, I wish…things could've been different." Nick looked away.

"You did your best. Sophia loved you, looked up to you. I know she did." Paco's dark eyes stayed on him.

"Well, I'm fortunate -- this girl, named Grace, she's helping me with everything. She's like an angel, you know?" Nick glanced Paco's way. He seemed busy cooking.

"Yeah. I know her. She's the ER doc, and she works at the shelter sometimes."

"Really? Huh. She never mentioned that." Nick responded.

"How do you know her?" Paco was stirring something that smelled wonderful.

"The first time I met her she treated me in the ER for that punch in the face. That was pretty embarrassing. A group of us went white water rafting for Paul's bachelor party on Labor Day Weekend. Grace was there in a cabin with her friends. I had no idea she'd be there. She's an amazing woman…" Nick's voice trailed off.

"You *did* her, didn't you? And, now you're madly in love, I can tell."

"What do you mean?" Nick felt himself becoming defensive.

"Doesn't matter what you call it. You did the horizontal Mambo, man. And, now you think just because *that* happened, she's going to feel the same way about you."

"Damn it, Paco. It wasn't like that. I didn't just have sex with her. This was *special*."

Paco laughed, "Oh okay. But, there's more to the story. She's hooked up with some dude, and you're second fiddle."

"Yeah. That's how it is." Nick was amazed at his power of perception. "How the hell did you know that?"

"Listen Nick. You can't make a chick love you. Trust me. I tried. If she wants you, she wants you. If she doesn't, then it's a waste of your time. Move on."

He put a plate of food on the counter before him. The aroma was delightful and Nick watched as Paco put salsa on his quesadilla, then sour cream and shredded lettuce. After the first bite, Nick almost choked as he took a drink of cold water.

"What the hell did you put in these? They're hot!"

"Aw, you're a pussy. That's all. This is good stuff." Paco laughed.

Nick realized that was the first time he ever heard Paco laugh. His friend seemed relaxed, and for the first time in a long time, the homeless veteran was probably feeling secure.

"So, I should *stop* chasing this chick?" Nick couldn't believe he was discussing his love life with Paco.

"No. Chase her, do all that you can to communicate your feelings. Guys don't do too well with that – you know? *Feelings*. Don't hold back, man. But, know this: you are laying your heart out there and it could possibly get crushed. Be prepared for anything. But my philosophy is: nothing ventured, nothing gained. Live your bucket list, man. Don't hold back."

For a second, Nick realized that Paco was more than an informant. He was a wise man, a friend, a psychologist of sorts, and a philosopher. Not only that, but he was an excellent dog handler, a good cook, and a talented photographer. Nick glanced around the place as he observed the enlarged photos of Diesel gracing the walls.

"These are amazing." Nick said between bites. "You have talent, amigo."

"I like doing it. They enlarged them at Staples. Didn't cost much, I got a veteran's discount. But, enough about me. You need to talk to anyone? I'm here, man. Whatever you need, just tell me. If you just want to unload, you can just sit here and talk. I'll listen."

"I appreciate that, Paco. I'll get through this, one day at a time, with the grace of God."

Paco smiled. "I like that. *The grace of God.* You're a good guy, Nick. When I first met you, I noticed you had eyes like Grace, pale blue eyes. You are both good people, filled with hope and truth. No bullshit, you know? You really care. You don't just pretend to care. You live it."

Nick's heart was warmed by the salsa and the compliment. Coming from Paco, that meant a lot. Praise, coming from a guy who'd been through so much himself, was sort of ironic. Nick felt he should be the one commending Paco, especially now that he knew more about him.

Chapter 10

Grace Robertson sat on the reception sofa at Doctor Child's office. She'd been seeing her therapist for the past eight months. In fact, it was Doctor Child who told her about the opening at Cherryfield General Hospital and the psychologist helped Grace build a life for herself, one week at a time. The door opened and Grace stared at the floor as Doctor Child walked a distraught-looking young woman to the outside door. A few words were exchanged, and Doctor Child turned her attention to Grace.

"Lunchtime. Come on, I have chicken salad."

Her smile was genuine and she wore horn-rimmed glasses, that were so outdated they'd come back in style. Her mismatched clothes and well-worn tennis shoes revealed much about her therapist. She was comfortable enough in her own skin to help other people sort out their messy lives.

Grace followed Doctor Child into the office and closed the door behind her. In a tiny fridge behind her desk, Grace watched as her therapist took out a sandwich and laid napkins atop her desk.

"You know me well enough now; you can call me Cee-Cee."

The doctor narrowed her eyes and her lips curved into the beginning of a smile. Her mocha skin and long dark wavy hair flattered her.

"Let's talk about this Michael Dean situation." Cee-Cee's big brown eyes stared into Grace's.

"He showed up on my front steps late at night. He's getting divorced. He's living here in Connecticut on the ocean and has a job as a cardiologist. I'm the cause of his divorce…" Grace began.

Cee-Cee stopped her mid-sentence. "No. You're not responsible for *his* actions."

Grace's brow furrowed. She sure *felt* responsible. If she'd never made love to Michael, none of this would've happened.

Cee-Cee frowned. "I'll be damned if I'm going to let you get tangled up with this dude because you feel *guilty* about his divorce. I'm just saying, he knew *exactly* what he was doing and he is the one who is responsible for his divorce. That's if it even materializes."

And, so the session went, between bites of chicken salad and a can of Pepsi, Grace and Cee-Cee went back and forth over the same territory she'd covered for the last eight months. Everything Cee-Cee said made perfect sense. Grace soaked in her wisdom and wondered how the hell Cee-Cee knew so much about this subject. But, then, she had been a therapist for many years and had been through a divorce herself. She had a boyfriend now, but he wasn't a live-in. He, too, was a therapist and they went to dog shows together and collected fine art. It seemed the life that Cee-Cee lived was far removed from Grace's.

She made another appointment when the hour was up and thanked Cee-Cee for her good advice, knowing full well it was the wisest course for her to take. If only she could put Cee-Cee in her pocket like a good-luck charm, or a worry stone ~ something to touch to help her remember exactly what she needed to do when the time came and she was alone.

* * *

Michael Dean paced back and forth in front of an enormous plate glass window overlooking a stunning view of the Atlantic Ocean with a martini in his hand. His plan was to have Grace there with him, but his strategy hadn't gone as he imagined. For some reason, she had pulled away and he wondered if there was another guy in her life. If there was, he wasn't on her Facebook page. He had checked on a friend's computer at the college, several times. He'd seen the photos of the bungalow and the pictures of her girlfriends in Cherryfield. Grace had managed to put him behind her and was making a new life for herself.

The cardiology practice had welcomed him and pressed him to move up the date to join. They had more patients than they could handle. When asked about his personal life, he'd lied. He said his wife would stay in New York to handle the sale of the house and his children wanted to transfer at the mid-point in the school year, if possible. It wasn't completely a lie. If Grace wouldn't allow him into her life, he imagined that could be how it really might go.

He dialed Grace's number again and it went to voicemail. She had to be on the phone with someone. He'd already texted her numerous times, but nothing. He began to wonder if this was going to be much more difficult than he had planned. Four years of his life was spent hiding in the shadows with Grace, taking her surreptitiously to conferences and seminars, even meeting her for spring break once. Ah, the treasured memories of that vacation he'd never forget. The small casita was a standalone unit on a private stretch of a white sand beach. Every so often he'd take out the photographs and examine them. She was incredibly beautiful, every inch of her. The other guys she'd dated were students, pot-heads or frat boys more interested in partying than in treating her like the woman she was. But, in retrospect, he was thankful the other men in her life had been so juvenile.

He remembered how she sat in the front row in the lecture hall. He'd never been so distracted in his life. The first few times she'd come to his office with questions after class, he had all he could do to stay in the role of her professor. Professor of what? Lust? Love? The first time he made love to her, it was amazing. She did everything, exactly as he wanted her to. She was compliant, but enthusiastic, eager to learn. From that moment on, he became obsessed with Grace. Any free time was devoted to meeting her, making love, even if it was in his office bathroom at the campus. Risky, yes. Worth it, always.

When Jeanine found the spring break photos, he was forced to tell her about the affair. He pleaded with her, but she made him sleep in the guest room for months. Finally, Jeanine announced she wanted a divorce. Although it wasn't the way he thought it would go, he didn't fight with her. The difficult part was the tremendous financial sacrifice he was making. Yes, the kids hated him, too. But, soon that would change – or so, he hoped. Their friends' parents were all divorced or on their third marriage by now. It wasn't such a big deal nowadays. They'd get over it. He had lived his life for his family for twenty years. *Now it was his time.*

But, *why*, after such a torrid love affair would Grace just end it? She'd threatened to leave him a couple of times, but he knew what to say to convince her to stay. She had even dated another guy, some shrimp named Jeremy. He didn't last long. Jeremy couldn't make her feel the way he did. The relationship he had with Grace was special. This was that once-in-a-lifetime kind of thing. He got what he wanted and Grace did, too. Few couples could say that.

He would continue trying to talk with her. Cherryfield General was a short drive away. He'd visit her there. If he had to camp out in front of her house, he'd do that, too. Eventually, she'd make eye contact with him and cave in to his demands.

Michael Dean showered and was too tired to shave before going to bed. He'd rise before the sun came up. He had surgery tomorrow morning and lots to do after that. He hadn't planned on changing jobs at age 45, but Grace had caused this. Now that he was free, he could focus all his attention on Grace and his new career. *Nothing else mattered.*

As he tapped his phone one last time, he realized she wasn't going to answer – not yet. Lunch time tomorrow, before he had to make rounds. He'd swing by Cherryfield General. One of the nurses there had given the schedule of the ER doctors to one of his coworkers at the practice. Thus, he knew Grace would be working tomorrow during the daytime.

Sleep was what he needed, but another martini and an hour later he tossed and turned. Eventually, he drifted into slumber. He contemplated Grace's smile as he walked through the door of her office at work. Seeing him in person would be much different than seeing him on a security camera. He made a mental note to bring street clothing to change into. She loved that gray cashmere sweater. He plotted how long it would take to drive to Cherryfield and back to the Metro Hospital in West Haven, maybe an hour tops. She loved cheese steak, he'd found a little place in Cherryfield that made a wonderful one just like the ones they used to eat in New York. *Yes. Soon, she'd be back in his arms and his world would be filled with love once again.*

Chapter 11

Not going to work was an odd feeling for Nick. He had worked non-stop since he'd started with the police force. Not seeing his brothers every day was a strange feeling. He felt alone, adrift. His mind filled with thoughts he didn't want to linger.

Sophia's death had conjured his mother's spirit and all the sad memories that came with it. Often his mother would come home drunk from a bar while Nick was making dinner for his siblings. As a young teenager, food stamps, coupons, a shopping cart that rolled home with him, became his daily routine. He tried to get the food stamps before his mother could trade them for alcohol and cigarettes. When she was drunk, she called him every name imaginable, and made up new ones. The verbal abuse he could take all day long, but the physical was another thing. She hit him over the head with a chair and he made an escape. Whenever she got that way, he'd hide in the basement and kill rats. The hardest part was protecting his younger siblings. He remembered the time Sophia was grabbed by one of his mother's intoxicated boyfriends. Nick punched the guy's face in, knocking out his front teeth. The policeman that responded that night had taken Nick aside. He remembered how calm the officer was when he told Nick he'd done the right thing, even though it was violent and dangerous. He said he would've done the same to protect his sister. That was the moment Nick knew he wanted to be like that man ~ in charge, in control, kind, and helpful. That was the first time he wanted to be a police officer.

Nick left his phone on the kitchen table and searched through his closet. The small box that held the photographs of his mother resided there and he sifted through them. She was a beautiful woman when she was young. But, over time, the smoking and drinking took its toll. Her health declined. Nick found it painful to look at the photographs now. He tucked them back into the box and found the ones of Sophia. He put them inside an envelope and left it on the table.

His phone vibrated and it was Aunt Brenda. She gave him an update on the time of arrival for his brothers, Victor and Alex. His sister, Natalie, was taking time off from school, too. They'd all arrive on Thursday. Nick double-checked to make sure she paid their air fare with the money he sent to her.

"You all right, Nicky?" his aunt asked.

"Yeah. I'll be over there on Thursday. I have some money to give you for flowers. You can order those, right? How're the girls doing with the photographs? I found some. I can bring them over. I've scanned them into my computer and you can keep them."

"Thank you." Brenda's voice was halting and he knew she was beginning to cry again.

"Yeah. It's okay. It'll all be okay." He disconnected the call. *No more crying.*

When he glanced at his phone, he noticed Paul had called him. Nick returned the call, suddenly remembering Paul's wedding was coming up.

"Hey, Nick. You doing okay? I'm sorry about Sophia. That was a horrible accident." Being a fireman, Paul was no stranger to gruesome scenes. He spent time in Cherryfield Community College with Nick and they'd become the closest of friends.

"Yeah, I'm okay. Just off work for a few days. I'd rather be working; you know?" Nick was being truthful.

"You still okay to be my best man? I'd understand if you couldn't because of what's happened. You've been through a lot the last couple of days." Paul had genuine concern in his voice.

"Yes, I'll be there. I've been fitted for the tux and will pick it up Saturday. The rehearsal dinner is Saturday night, if I remember correctly." Nick was peering at his calendar hanging on the fridge.

"Friday's the day of your sister's service. I read it in the newspaper and someone posted it on Facebook." Paul lingered, giving him a last chance to pull out. "You know, Cooper said he'd stand-in for you if you're not up to it."

"Nah. Don't worry. I can't miss your wedding. Sophia's service is a luncheon thing. My brothers and sisters will be there, maybe a few others. I will make it to your rehearsal dinner on Saturday. No worries. I'll see you then, Paul. Thanks for calling."

After dropping the photographs off at his aunt's house, he drove by Cherryfield General and the Land Rover was in the reserved space. He sprang out of his Jeep and zipped his fleece jacket that had Cherryfield Police Department lettered on the back. The reception area of the ER was half-filled with incoming patients and family members drumming their fingers, waiting patiently for a nurse to approach them with some bit of information.

Nick spotted Trish and she walked over to him.

"Hey, Nick, I'm sorry about Sophia." She unexpectedly embraced him and he was speechless for a moment. His eyes moved above Trish's shoulder and he spotted the figure of a man talking to Grace at the doorway of her office. The guy wasn't dressed in hospital garb, but street clothes, a gray cashmere sweater that looked expensive. The way he moved closer to Grace and leaned in made Nick think this was someone familiar. She was smiling up at the guy and seemed happy to see him. It looked like he was handing her something in a bag.

"Who's that?" Nick asked Trish.

"Oh, you mean him? The guy talking to Grace, I mean Doctor Robertson? I think he said his name was Doctor Dean. Maybe he's consulting on a case with her. I've never seen him before."

"Yeah, okay."

Nick saw Grace laugh again. Whatever this dude was saying must've been pretty funny.

"I need to talk with her. I'm going to be having lunch with her. She's off right now, isn't she?" Nick asked.

"Yes, good timing."

Trish whisked another patient through the double doors. Nick strode confidently down the hallway. As he approached, the man's back was to him. Grace saw Nick first. She seemed startled.

"Nick! Hi… didn't expect you." She stammered.

As Doctor Dean spun around, Nick extended his hand to the muscled gray-haired man. Within a few seconds Nick took in the details of this stranger. He looked nearly old enough to be Grace's father. Tanned skin, a golfer or tennis player, no doubt. Nick noticed a little bit of five o'clock shadow and caught the aroma of an expensive cologne. The sweater certainly made a statement, it was too tight and looked ridiculous on him.

"Hey, I'm Nick Kozlovsky. Great to meet you – and you are?" Nick looked him square in the eye.

There was something about the man he instinctively did not like. His eyes met Nick's then averted, usually the sign of a shifty bastard. He stood about six-one and Nick guessed he weighed about 180. Not any excess weight; he spent time in the gym to stay in that kind of shape. The man had silvery cropped hair and teeth that were bleached too white.

"Oh, hello there. I'm Doctor Michael Dean, an old friend of Grace's. We go way back to college days. Right Grace?"

Nick detected alcohol on his breath. Vermouth, to be exact. It had an odor that was repugnant.

The way this guy looked at Grace repulsed him. *It was the same way the drunk guy looked at Sophia just before Nick punched his teeth out.* But, Nick did not give away his feelings. He smiled and moved past Michael Dean into Grace's small private office, pushing the smaller man aside with his sheer size.

"We're having lunch, Doctor Dean, so if you'll excuse us."

Nick drove him further into the hallway and closed the office door in Dean's bewildered face. He sensed the guy was pissed. But the surprise of his quick action broke the spell he had with Grace.

Nick listened as Michael Dean's footsteps resonated in the hallway. Grace exhaled a noticeable sigh of relief.

"Wow, talk about good timing." She uttered.

"So, *that's* the guy."

"What do you mean?" Grace glanced his way, and Nick knew she was feigning innocence.

"The guy who has your attention right now." Nick didn't want to sound antagonistic, but realized he probably was.

Grace sat at her desk and opened the wrapper on her sandwich. "I don't know what you're talking about."

"I'm sorry. It's just that you seem distracted since the rafting trip. I hope I didn't do anything…." But Nick couldn't finish his sentence.

"No. No. That was…awesome. I mean, it was wonderful. I'm distracted by my work more than anything. I'm new as an ER doc, you know. No two days are ever the same." She gushed.

"Yeah. I know the feeling. Police work is the same way." Nick's eyes locked with hers. *Yes, she was still interested. The way her eyes lingered and held his, he could tell.*

Nick continued, "I'd been trying to get in touch with you about Paul's wedding. Saturday afternoon is the rehearsal dinner. Then, Sunday morning is the ceremony, it's at a fancy oceanfront resort. I'm the best man. I was hoping you'd come with me to the wedding. I'm working both nights; I think you are, too. I glanced at the schedule on my way in…"

"Yes, I'd love to." Grace smiled. "Would you like half of this sandwich? It's huge!"

Nick pulled up a wooden chair and sat across from her. "Yes, I'm starving."

Although he couldn't get any information from her regarding Michael Dean, she talked about Sophia's wake and asked again if she could help in any way. Nick would never let on that another couple of thousand was piled on top of the already overused credit card that resided in his wallet.

When finished, she stood up and washed her hands in the small sink in her office. Nick watched as she brushed her teeth and rinsed with mouthwash. After she applied lipstick, she turned to face him.

"I'm sorry, but my lunch break is over." Grace moved toward the door.

He moved closer until he left her no room at all.

"Thank you, Grace." Her eyes met his and he instantly kissed her, tasting the spearmint mouthwash. He wanted more, but held himself in check. Instead, Nick placed his hand on the door handle and opened it. As she walked through, he noticed Grace was smiling. He now wanted to know everything about Michael Dean and what he was doing in Grace's office and at her house.

Even though he was off duty, on the way home Nick drove through his sector. He pulled the Jeep into the back of Strictly Storage and Paco opened the door.

"Hey, I've got something for you." Paco whispered. Nick stepped inside and Paco showed him a series of photographs he'd taken from the day before. Nick sent the photos to his phone and erased them from Paco's.

"Good work." Nick sighed.

"You're tired, amigo. And, you had a mix-up with the other guy. I can tell by the look on your face. You don't think you have a chance with her, do you?"

"How the hell do you *know* that?" Nick laughed.

"It's written all over your face. You don't think you're good enough for Grace."

"Really?"

"Yes. But you *are* the right guy for her. You have the same things in common. You are kind and caring and want to make the world a better place. She does, too. You're a good man, Nick. She's a lucky woman to have you. Just because this other dude has money, doesn't mean shit. It's what's in his heart that counts. He'll never beat you on that count. Now get out of here. I don't want anyone to see me talking with a cop."

* * *

Paco took Diesel out for a walk. It was dark and almost time for the methadone clinic to close. He didn't have far to walk and Diesel trotted by his side knowing where they were headed. Paco had found a dog harness that fit Diesel perfectly. It was left in a storage unit that went unpaid for sixty days. The owner told him to sort through the stuff, toss what looked like trash or sell it on Craig's List. It was a treasure trove for Paco. He found a few pots and pans, some silverware to pawn and books to read.

The patrol officer filling in for Nick had already made a pass through the neighborhood. The wind was colder tonight and Paco remembered the nights he shivered in the tent. Now he felt like a king. How life could turn around. A year ago, he was contemplating suicide. That was when Diesel wandered into his life. A month ago, he was homeless and at the end of his resources. That was when Nick handed him a twenty-dollar bill.

For the first time in a long time, Paco felt his life had a specific purpose. He stepped up his pace. He wanted to make it to the clinic before closing time. He didn't think anything of the car parked in front of the building as he walked through the glass door with Diesel. And, he didn't really think too much about how odd Diesel acted about going inside. The dog literally pulled Paco back toward the entry door.

"What's the matter, boy?" Paco gave his full attention to Diesel. "You gotta pee? Okay, back outside we go."

Diesel tugged on the harness and they were outside and 50 feet along the side of the building when Paco heard the sound. It was all too familiar, that pop-pop-pop of a semi-auto handgun. He crouched in the darkness behind some shrubs and Diesel nestled against him. The vehicle that had been idling was in view. Paco watched as two men jumped into it. The tires spun and left rubber on the pavement. Squealing and steering wildly, the dark sedan took a left onto Parkway and disappeared.

Paco tapped his phone and called 911. After giving a description of the vehicle, he wondered if Tammy was okay inside the clinic. Paco scrambled with Diesel to get inside, but the door was locked. Tammy might have somehow triggered the lockdown mechanism. As he stood at the curb, a squad car pulled up, then another, and another, lights blinding him.

"What happened? Did you see?" A policeman yelled to Paco.

Paco gave the description of the vehicle and the officer spoke into his radio.

"Where were you standing?" the cop asked him.

"Right over there. My dog had to pee. I was just stopping by. I'm a patient here. This is my regular time to stop in." Paco explained.

Meanwhile, Paco noticed the cops had managed to get the door to the clinic to open. He watched helplessly as an ambulance arrived and EMT's raced inside. He wondered what happened in there, but a cop pushed him aside when he attempted to enter the building.

"Sorry, pal."

Paco ran to the stretcher as it wheeled toward the ambulance. "Is she okay?"

"She's been shot. Move aside."

The EMT was on a radio calling Cherryfield General Emergency Room. Paco stood on the curb as the ambulance pulled away at warp speed, lights flashing, siren blaring. He prayed that Tammy would be all right. He tapped his phone but the call went to Nick's voicemail.

"Hey, it's me. I need to talk with you."

Paco hung up the phone and waited, but no one came to reopen the clinic and he'd missed his methadone dose tonight. He had already started sweating, and had become tired and anxious. He knew he had enough of the drug in his body to carry him through the night and even into the next day. But after that, he'd be vomiting and the diarrhea would start if he didn't get a dose.

Back at his small home, he drank several glasses of water because he knew the sweats could dehydrate him to the point of coma. Paco steeled himself for a long night. Late in the evening, he heard a tap on the door and Diesel's tail wagged. He squinted through the peep hole and saw Nick on his doorstep. Paco opened the door and Nick slipped inside.

"Don't worry. I parked out back. I got your message. What's up?" Nick asked.

"Shooting at the clinic tonight. I was going in to get my dose, as usual, but Diesel kept pulling me toward the door. He damn near dragged me outside. That's when I heard the gunfire. Tammy, they hauled her away in the wagon. I gotta find out if she's okay. Can you call Grace?"

Paco noticed Nick was staring at him.

"Paco, are you okay? I mean, you're shaking."

Paco hesitated, then spoke matter-of-factly.

"I never got my dose. I'll be okay tonight. I can get my dose in the morning. The clinic opens early." He felt like a loser telling Nick about his habit. But, Nick said something that surprised him.

"Have you ever thought of detoxing?"

"Yeah, I have. Actually, tried it a couple of times. I couldn't get past the fourth day. It's awful, man. You feel like you have the flu on steroids. But, it's so much worse than just hurling and crapping. The tremors, the nightmares, the sweats, the pain– then after that, I was so tired. My body shut down."

"Try to get through tonight. Tomorrow morning you can go over there and get a dose. You saw this whole thing go down? Did you give a statement to the police?" Nick asked.

"Yes. I called 911. They took my statement. The weird thing was, there was a guy in the car, it was running. He looked at me and I looked back at him as Diesel pulled me through the door. I've *seen* that dude before. He's trouble."

"You told the police that, right?"

"Yeah."

"Anything I can get for you before I leave? I mean, other than methadone?" Nick touched his arm.

"Yeah, this is gonna sound crazy, but I need sugar. Could you get me some Orange Crush or some grape juice, something like that? Get a couple." Paco sat down on the couch, thankful Nick was there to help him.

"Anything else?" Nick looked into Paco's dark eyes.

"Yeah, if you can get me some marijuana. It helps, believe it or not."

"Okay, I'll be right back. Can't make any promises on the marijuana." Nick closed the door.

Paco bolted the door and looked down at Diesel. "Gonna be a rough night, boy." Diesel's tail wagged and Paco sat on the floor and hugged him.

* * *

Stop 'N Shop was closed, so Nick went to the Quick-Save on the corner. A group of young people had congregated in front of the place and Nick's eyes roamed over the group quickly. He recognized some of them. Inside, he grabbed an armload of orange, grape, whatever he could find for Paco. Then he spotted the girls and tried to avoid their eyes, but it was too late.

"Nicky! What are you doing in here?" Kristie nearly screamed. Beth and Lexi were with her and they joined in. "Nick, you're off tonight?"

He tried to think of a way to get rid of them.

"Yeah, my sister died, or didn't you know?"

Kristie was next to him as he put the soft drinks in half liter bottles onto the counter. Then, Beth and Lexi sidled up to him.

"We're sorry about Sophia. She was hanging with Taylor and some bad guys, Nick. We couldn't stop her. We tried."

Nick finished paying the cashier. "Gotta go."

"Where are you going?" Kristie was insistent. The three girls followed him outside. Nick got into his Jeep, waved and drove away.

After dropping off the sugary soft drinks to Paco, Nick headed home. He hoped Paco wouldn't be found in the morning on the floor in a diabetic coma. He wondered if it was possible to drink too much sugar.

He backed the Jeep into his space in the driveway and approached his back door.

Kristie, Beth and Lexi jumped out of the darkness, "Surprise!"

"Damn it! Don't do that to a guy with a gun."

"Sorry, Nicky!"

"Shh---you'll wake up the whole house." Nick couldn't believe they were so bold. It was the alcohol, no doubt. All three of them had been clubbing and not too steady on their feet. He knew Kristie had been driving, *not* a good idea. He opened the door to his apartment and the girls filed in, immediately stepping out of their three-inch heels. Kristie was already all over him, tugging at his shirt, pulling him toward the unmade bed.

Nick sat on the bed and put his head in his hands for a moment. He had to get them out of there, *somehow.*

"Look, I don't feel so good. This friend of mine has the flu and was vomiting. Now I think I might have caught it. I feel like I'm going to be sick."

Nick ran his hand over his abdomen and winced.

Beth placed her hand on his forehead. "You do feel kind of hot."

Nick looked into her eyes. She wore too much eye make-up and her pupils were dilated. She was legally drunk. Beth and Lexi were even more intoxicated.

"Listen, Kristie – sick or not -- I've gotta take you girls home. You *can't* drive like this." Her hand was touching his cheek and she leaned in to kiss him, but Nick gently pushed her away.

"Come on, ladies. We're going for a ride in my Jeep."

Nick led them to the driveway. He collected Kristie's car keys and helped the girls buckle up. For the next forty minutes, he drove through the streets of Cherryfield as he dropped off Lexi, then Kristie. Beth was the last one.

"I wanna go home with you, Nicky…" Her speech was slurred and Nick caught a whiff of her breath. *Ugh.*

"No, Beth. You're going home, too. Give me the address again. If you don't I can find out. So, just tell me."

Reluctantly, Beth turned her face away.

"It's 15 Garfield…apartment 4A."

"Right."

It was midnight by the time he got back to his apartment.

The old Nick might have taken advantage of Kristie, Lexi, or Beth – or possibly all three of them. But lately, it was as if he was having an out of body experience observing himself. He didn't want to be that guy any more, the one who pulled the clothing off a pretty girl who was drunk and begging him to do so. Lots of times he'd done it. Many a night he was nearly asleep, and remembered opening one eye as he tried to focus on the alarm clock. The door creaked shut as what's-her-name left. His eyes fluttered. He didn't lose any sleep. Casual sex. He hated the thought of it now. It no longer filled his needs. The euphoria of hedonism stopped his self-loathing only for a short time. Love was what he yearned for, and he knew Grace had lots of love, but was her heart still attached to Michael Dean?

When he woke at 9 AM, his eyes remained closed as he gradually realized daylight was filtering through the window. He felt pleased that he had kept the pact with himself – no more casual sex – period. And, for once, he felt a smidgeon of pride run through him. He wanted more than anything to live up to the high standards Grace had unknowingly set for him. He wanted to be her blue knight.

He remembered the guys who went skulking out in the wee hours of the morning from his mother's room. Sometimes they'd made eye contact with him briefly, then looked away. Nick imagined they felt embarrassed. These strange men were uncomfortable looking into the eyes of a nine-year old boy who knew the truth. But, it hurt Nick more to see them leaving like that. Love wasn't supposed to be something you were ashamed of. In the movies or on television, women and men kissed and held hands. There was love involved long before the sex act. He never remembered seeing a man kiss his mother or hold her hand. And he learned early on it was because they didn't love her. They used her. And, now he was trying to escape the same trap. While the erotic romp took place, it felt like love. But, later, the memory of it turned sour and made him feel empty inside. He realized this was what his mother felt like, too, except she had a hangover to top it off. No wonder she was depressed.

He hastily made coffee and took a shower. The coffee cup slipped out of his clumsy paw onto the tile floor. It shattered into what seemed like a hundred shards. He told himself the cup represented the old Nick. As he swept it up, he remembered he was supposed to be at his Aunt

Brenda's for Sophia's service. He bolted to the closet to find his suit. He had no idea how many people would show up, or if anyone other than family would attend. The charcoal gray suit and blue necktie were reserved for funerals and weddings. Unfortunately, he'd attended many more funerals. He collected his car keys and phone, then dabbed a bit of cologne on his hands and ran them through his hair. No time to get pretty.

Chapter 12

Grace pulled her hair back and applied a soft natural lipstick. She had many little black dresses in her closet and decided on a conservative one with a matching jacket. Michael had been calling and texting her, but she had to support Nick in his time of crisis. Grace knew Nick was putting on a good front for his family. As she drove to his aunt's house, she recalled driving by his house late last night. She was thinking he'd be sad and lonely. But when she saw three young women getting into his Jeep, she kept on driving. She didn't want to assume anything, but it didn't look like he was lonely.

As she walked through the back door of the two-family dwelling, she noticed Nick's aunt in the kitchen giving orders to two teenage girls. Photos of Sophia were everywhere, and an enlarged one of her smiling was in the parlor along with her ashes in a small urn.

"Welcome, thank you for coming."

Aunt Brenda was warm and introduced herself and then Nick's youngest siblings, Julia and Katie. Natalie, Victor and Alex were standing shoulder to shoulder in front of an old buffet and each shook her hand. Grace felt a tap on her shoulder and turned to view Nick in a gray suit with a tie. As she pivoted to face him, Grace felt her face flush with warmth.

"I'm sorry for your loss, Nick." Grace felt silly saying those words. She really wanted to tell him she thought he was a wonderful person, and he didn't deserve this heartbreak. She wanted to say he'd been through enough and she wanted nothing more than to comfort him. Although she didn't say it, she felt Nick could hear her secret thoughts.

He embraced her and she felt his lips on her ear. "Thank you for coming."

Within the next few minutes the house filled up with young women. Grace noticed several who sent long, private glances Nick's way and he intentionally ignored them. One was a tall blonde wearing a body-hugging dress. She had the figure of a gazelle and her eyes never left Nick for a minute. Another young woman, who introduced herself as Beth, also spent time standing near Nick and chatting with him whenever possible. The third girl was very young, maybe still a teenager, and Grace thought she heard the name Lexi. Assuming they were friends of Sophia's, Grace tried not to assign too much importance to their interest in Nick. Still, it bothered her how they clung to him, their hands touching his arm or his back in a familiar way. For a second, a nauseating feeling flooded through Grace. What if Nick was a ladies' man, a hound dog? He couldn't be! Not with that baby face and those clear blue eyes. And, he was a Boy Scout, too.

Ten minutes later, a sea of blue arrived. Cooper, Herrick, Johnson, the list was endless. One by one, each police officer gave their deepest condolences and shook Nick's hand and that of each sibling. Aunt Brenda was in tears. Their presence somehow brought a sense of dignity to Sophia's passing. Grace's heart warmed as she observed the tender scene.

Nick was so happy to see them. They loved Nick. He was part of them. This was his real family, the force, and all that it stood for – justice, decency, hope – something deep, and true blue.

By 4 PM, the visitors filed out and only the family members remained. Nick stood next to Grace at the kitchen counter and the two of them finished off the remainder of a delicious platter of food from Lentini's. Grace could tell by looking at

Nick's face he was relieved it was over. He hugged his aunt and siblings and tugged Grace toward the driveway.

"Take me home with you." He whispered as the sun started to slip toward the horizon.

Grace hesitated for a moment, then feeling reckless, answered, "Okay."

She watched Nick's Jeep in her rearview mirror as she pulled into the driveway of her small residence. But as she approached, she noticed the black Jaguar parked in front of her house and her stomach knotted with anxiety. As she pulled into the driveway, Nick pulled in behind her. She stepped out of her vehicle and Nick was instantly at her side.

"You want me to get rid of him?" Nick offered calmly.

Grace hesitated as her eyes darted toward Michael. She could feel him watching.

"No. I don't want any trouble. I've got to talk with him. You should go."

"Who is this dude to you? What business does he have showing up unannounced?"

"He's an old boyfriend." Grace didn't want to get into the details.

"Yeah, he's too old for you, if you ask me. The guy looks like he could be your father."

Grace knew Nick was right, but felt herself defending Michael Dean. "He left his wife."

"What? This guy is *married*?"

Grace dropped her eyes to the ground, suddenly filled with shame. "Yes."

"You're making a big mistake, Grace, you realize that, don't you?"

She felt Nick's finger beneath her chin and his eyes on her upturned face. Reluctantly, her eyes met his. She could see the calm fury residing there. And, she instantly knew Nick would remove Michael Dean from her life, if she gave him the signal. *But she didn't.*

"Let me handle this. I don't want any drama." Grace put her hand on Nick's chest. He looked so handsome in that suit. Surprising her, she felt Nick lean down and kiss her. His lips brushed against hers and she sensed his longing to protect her.

"Don't let him inside." Nick whispered. "Talk out here, in the driveway. Text me when he leaves."

Grace watched Nick climb into his Jeep and pull away, but before he did, she noticed he glared in the direction of the Jaguar. She hoped she had made the right decision, but wondered if she had. As soon as Nick was out of sight, Michael got out of the Jaguar and approached her in the driveway.

"Good, he's gone." He smiled. "I didn't want to interrupt your conversation. It looked a little intense."

Grace tried to avoid his gaze, but was unsuccessful. His deep-set gray eyes fixed intently on her face. She felt Michael's hand on her arm as he ushered her toward the door.

"We need to talk, my love."

* * *

Nick glanced in the rearview mirror as he pulled away and saw Michael Dean walk toward Grace in the driveway. What was he saying to her?

What sort of relationship did she have with this guy? The dude was married, that was trouble right there. Nick was fuming. He didn't want to think of Grace with a guy like that. He was obviously a wolf, playing around with her, and he already had a wife. Nick needed to talk to someone about this predicament, and Paco came to mind.

His Jeep cruised to the other side of town to Paco's humble dwelling and Nick tapped on the door after parking behind a storage unit in the back. It took a few minutes, but Paco opened the door. He looked like he hadn't slept.

"Hey, you okay?" Nick queried.

"Yeah. It's the methadone. I'm kickin' it, man. Get in here."

Nick moved through the door and bolted it. "What can I do to help?"

"I had accumulated a large amount of the drug in my system. Day one wasn't too bad. But now I'm on day two. I'm getting jittery, uncomfortable. Horrible pains throughout my body, fatigue, and the most painful part is my legs. I took Advil, it was useless. I'm having these nightmares and wake up every five minutes. I know what the next two days will bring. I've got to get some marijuana. That's the only way I'll sleep."

"I'll see what I can do to help. What happens if I can't get it?"

"After a few more days, I will be in the deepest darkest crevice of hell, lying on my bed in a fetal position crying and shaking."

"You can't just kick methadone. You need a reduced dose every day. Maybe I should have checked you into the ER?"

"No. They wouldn't take me anyhow. And, I won't go. You know me, Nick, I'm a loner. I've got to do this by myself. I'm having the worst insomnia I've ever experienced. If I could temporarily amputate my legs, I would be happy. Nothing worse than tossing and turning because of pain."

Nick swallowed hard.

"Okay. When you told me you might do this, I got some information from a friend of mine. She's a nurse at the hospital. What *can* help, even if only for a few minutes, is a hot bath. The trick is to sit in it while it fills up extremely hot, that way you aren't reluctant to get in when you stick your toe in and feels too hot. Let the water warm up while your body is in it."

Paco looked pitiful.

"I'm a zombie, man, mentally exhausted from not sleeping. One time when I tried this, I was up for almost four days straight. That's why kickin' is so hard, can't sleep a wink. I was hoping that you'd show up today, man. I'm glad you did. I'm a total wreck. Hey, Nick – I need some Immodium for the runs."

"Okay. Let me get you into the tub and warmed up; get that pain to stop driving you crazy."

Nick went into the bathroom and prepared the bath for Paco. *What was he thinking?* He knew this was going to be difficult, if not impossible, for Paco. There was no way he could stay with him around the clock. He tapped his phone and dialed the ER, and asked for Trish.

"Yes, who is this? Nick?" Trish sounded concerned.

"Yeah. Listen. I have a huge favor to ask of you."

"Go on…"

Nick turned away as Paco stripped and moved into the tub as it filled. The glimpse of Paco's frail body was enough to let him know he wasn't eating enough. The drugs were kicking his ass. He knew it was a long shot, but if he could help Paco get off the drugs, maybe he had a chance to regain his health.

Nick sat on the commode as he gazed toward a shivering Paco. Diesel slipped into the bathroom and rested his head on the edge of the tub. Paco rubbed Diesel's ears.

"Listen, Paco. I've got a good friend. She's going to stop by on and off and help you through this. You need a dose every day, but it's a weaning process. She is a wonderful nurse. She knows the doctor at the clinic."

"Oh, no, man. I don't want any chick to see me like this. Or anyone, for that matter. I've got *some* dignity, you know." Paco murmured as the tremors overtook him.

"Please, do this for me. She'll bring you some food and medical supplies, along with that dose that will stop what's taking place in your intestines right now. Let her help you, please, Paco." Nick was desperate to gain his trust.

"Who is she?"

"Trish. A girl I know from the hospital. She's a nurse and she is fearless."

Nick held his breath for a moment. He could see that Paco was giving the idea some consideration.

After a moment, Paco nodded.

"Okay. Send her over. I'll do it. I've gotta kick this stuff. I'm making progress, but I know it's gonna get worse, and I'll need her help."

"Good. She'll be here in an hour."

"How the hell did you know I'd say *yes*?"

"I had a feeling you would." Nick smiled. "I don't want to look at your skinny ass. I'll be out here in the kitchen.

Nick moved through the door and Diesel followed him. As Nick sat on the sofa, Diesel hopped up and laid his head in his lap. Nick rubbed the canine's ears and thought about Paco. He hoped he could make it through the next few days. He imagined himself at Paul's rehearsal luncheon as Paco was suffering. He pictured himself enjoying Paul's wedding ceremony as Paco was in the deepest throes of withdrawal.

Twenty minutes later, Paco emerged. The tremors hadn't stopped, but were lessened. "My legs don't hurt as much."

"Yes. You've got to do that several times a day – and into the night." Nick suggested.

"Okay. It works better than any pain reliever I've taken."

"Good." Nick nodded. "Trish will bring you dinner, some soup from the deli. Eat, even though you feel nauseated. You need nutrition. She's going to bring you some supplements, too. She knows a lot about this stuff, Paco. You've got to trust her."

"I will. I got no alternative." Paco's dark eyes had a flicker of hope as they met Nick's. "Hey, man. Thanks."

* * *

Grace opened the door and Michael stepped over the threshold. She heard him close the door as she turned to hang her coat. It had been eight long months since she'd been alone with him and she tried to cover up the nervousness she felt inside. His hand brushed against hers as he reached to hang his coat on the hook and his body was inches away.

"I've missed you, Grace."

His deep mellow voice was all too familiar. Grace avoided looking at his handsome face, now with the stubble of a beginning beard. The silvery gray matched the thick hair on his head. He could've been right off the cover of GQ, ruggedly handsome, masculine. Grace felt her heartbeat quicken. She fought to maintain her composure.

"I'm surprised they allow you to have facial hair at Metro Cardiology."

It was all she could think of to say at that moment and realized how stupid she probably sounded. This conversation was going to take a turn for the worse very shortly. She doubted Michael would be too happy when he left. But, Cee-Cee's words were imprinted in her brain –

Don't let him in, Grace. You're finished with this guy. Be strong.

Grace felt Michael's eyes on her as she moved through the parlor into the kitchen.

"Water?"

"Sure."

His lean sinewy body leaned against the counter and her eyes swept over him. He looked the same. He might have lost a few pounds. He wore that gray cashmere sweater she loved. Why did he have to be so damned attractive? Why did he have to smell so good? Why were these thoughts running wildly through her brain? She knew Michael was undressing her with his eyes. She'd almost forgotten how efficient he was in the art of undressing. As much as she tried to push the memories away, they flooded through her mind in rapid succession.

That first time. He'd taken her into his office bathroom at the campus and locked the door. He'd ripped her blouse off her body and pulled her skirt down, ravishing her right there against the wall. He suckled her breasts and thrust his fingers into the warm, wet spot between her legs. She had never experienced anything like that before. The few boyfriends she'd been intimate with never dominated her in that way. He teased her to orgasm over and over for an hour ~ it was euphoric. Later that afternoon, her underwear was still lying on his bathroom floor as she sat in the front row of his class. She found herself sharing secret glances with Michael while sitting in the front row, crossing her legs, still wet from the encounter. She enjoyed the fact that he was struggling to concentrate on teaching. That was the first moment she thought she had control over him. She told herself that Michael was weak and she was powerful. And, for four years she lied to herself about how wonderful he was. But, as reality crept in – she realized her life was lonely and miserable, especially when he spent most of his free time with his wife and four children. Michael held all the power in the relationship. Grace's depression got so serious, she sought help, never realizing she held the key to the problem all along.

But now, she had to make Michael understand. She allowed her eyes to meet his only briefly. Already she could tell he was wildly excited to be in the same room with her. Grace couldn't allow herself to fall into the trap again, as Cee-Cee had put it.

"Please, Grace, don't push me away." Michael played the role of heartbroken lover expertly.

"Michael, I've got to talk. You've got to listen."

Grace had the kitchen island between them and felt as if she was in a fortress with Cee-Cee there to protect her.

Michael played the romantic card.

"You remember how you loved me, Grace? All the good times we had together? The conference in the Caribbean, making love in my office, all those dinners off campus in those little hideaways? I can't just forget about you...forget about us."

Grace trembled. In counseling sessions, she'd seen him for the monster he really was ~ a cheating husband, with a wife and four children, her professor, 15 years her senior. And, she knew she wasn't the only one he played around with – *there were others*. He'd lied to her all along. And, she was stupid enough to believe she was the only one. She tried to summon the words to tell Michael how it was over – truly over. She had practiced this speech so many times with Cee-Cee, but now her mind went blank.

He started to move around the island closer to her.

"You are mine – all mine – don't forget that, Grace. Your big ape of a friend won't do a thing to save you from me. He may have pushed me out of your office, but you *belong* to me, baby."

"Stop right there." Grace put her hand up, as if she was in control. At least she wanted to look the part. "There is no more *relationship* between us. It's in the past, and it's finished."

There, she said it. Michael turned away and Grace could tell he was thinking of what he could say to convince her. She'd been in this conversation before with him. He won that time. *But, now it was her turn to win.* Out of the corner of her eye, she noticed Michael was biting his lip. He always did that when he was nervous. Grace steadied herself for what she knew would come. She placed her hands on the kitchen island. The cold slab of marble mirrored what she felt in her heart. But, she had to communicate that to Michael, now, here, at this moment.

He moved closer to the end of the kitchen island. Grace knew he'd make a play for her. She sensed he'd wanted to when he came to her office with the sandwich, but there were too many people watching – and Nick pushed him out.

"Grace, I can't live without you."

A tear slid down his cheek as his face twisted with pain. Michael was at the point of crying and pleading. *Cee-Cee told her this would happen.*

His hand covered hers on the counter, but Grace pulled away.

"Don't do this, Michael."

He pulled his hand back and raked it through his hair, clearly frustrated.

"I'm sorry, babe. I just need you to *listen* to me. I feel as if you're a thousand miles away and I can't reach you."

"It's over, Michael. It's fruitless for you to stand here and go through this discussion. We've talked on the phone, you've texted me, messaged me on Facebook, to the point where I had to block this discussion out of my life. I'm blocking you out of my life, Michael. You have to accept it."

Grace thought that sounded about as direct and forthright as she could muster. Her stomach knotted and she wondered if he would leave willingly -- or if this was going to become a problem. *It all felt so senseless and sickeningly familiar. Cee-Cee was right. Nick was right. She hoped she wouldn't regret letting him inside to talk.*

"Let me touch you…I need to get through to you." Michael insisted. He'd stopped just short, now standing near her, but Grace moved to the far end of the kitchen island.

"If you don't leave me alone, Michael, there's going to be trouble. Legal trouble." Grace felt her voice waver. "I'll get a restraining order."

"My God, Grace! What happened to you?" Michael's face changed. She saw the flash of anger in his steely gray eyes.

Grace tried to remain composed, which was becoming more difficult the longer he was there. Then, he surprised her.

"I'm leaving, *for now*. I'm not going to fight with you. I understand you're angry with me, Grace. But, this isn't over."

She stood in the kitchen for a moment as she heard the front door close. The Jaguar hummed, then he drove away. Grace exhaled and the stress left her body. *Good.* The confrontation had taken place and she did everything Cee-Cee instructed her to do. Even though she put on a tough front, Grace didn't feel like she'd won. *What she really wanted was the four years back that she wasted on this pompous ass.* But, Cee-Cee had explained, you can never go back…only forward. Don't make the same mistake again. Cee-Cee spent an hour every week for eight months getting to know Grace. Even though Grace felt bulletproof when she sat in her therapy sessions, when she opened the door to Michael today, she felt panicky, fearful. She wondered if she could even *say* those things without crying and collapsing into his arms. And, even though she had done it, said the words, she had this nagging feeling that it *might not be over.*

Chapter 13

The night of his sister's wake was filled with loneliness and despair for Nick. If he had any semblance of a normal family, he would've spent it with them. But he wasn't close to his siblings. It was Grace who occupied his thoughts tonight. She had a way of uplifting his spirit. Just being in her presence would reassure him that all would be right with the world again. He craved her right now.

Although it was a chilly night, he revved the Harley and glided by Grace's house, sure she could hear the sound of the bike inside, unless…she was with him. Damn. Michael Dean's car was still parked in front. It had been there a while. His heart sank as he realized she had let the man inside. He hoped she wasn't involved with him, but knew he couldn't control Grace and her emotions, no more than he could control his own right now. *He loved her.* It seemed crazy and he knew it wasn't logical, but she was the one he wanted.

He wondered if she would ever want him. Grace was a doctor and Michael Dean was a doctor. They had that in common. But, at one time, Dean had been her med school professor. That smacked of sleaze right there. Any guy who'd use his position of power like that…to prey on a young, vulnerable girl…Nick had no respect for the man.

But, as he examined his own behavior over the past few years, he realized he wasn't much better than Michael Dean. Kristie, Beth, Lexi, and other girls spent time in his bedroom and he soaked in the adoration they showered upon him because he was a police officer in a uniform. How was he different than Michael Dean? He had tossed girls ten years younger than him into bed on a regular basis. As long as they were 18 years of age and willing, what the hell. But, since he'd met Grace, all of that had changed. She was different. Making love to her was…loving. His heart was involved.

He drove to Bud's Diner and noticed Trish's vehicle was at Paco's place. *Good, she was helping him.* Nick would owe her for this. Naomi, his usual waitress, locked her eyes on him the moment he walked through the door.

"Hey, Officer Kozlovsky, not on duty tonight?" She looked pretty cute in those black pants with a white shirt, unbuttoned so her cleavage showed. Nick tried not to stare.

"No, ma'am, but I'm hungry. Dinner and a root beer float tonight, Naomi."

She brought him to his usual table and served him with a smile. In street clothes, no one paid much attention to him; just another big guy in a leather jacket and jeans. But Naomi knew he was a cop and flirted with him every time he came to the restaurant. Until now, he hadn't noticed how much he had basked in her attention. He wasn't interested in her, but she fed his ego. He wondered if that's how Doctor Michael Dean felt with Grace. She had probably been one of his groupies when he was teaching at med school. He tried to banish the thought of Grace with Michael Dean. He wanted to think of Grace with *him*, and the night at the cabin.

As Naomi approached with the check, she leaned over, and like an idiot he looked down at her smooth skin.

"Would you like some company tonight?" she whispered.

Nick was taken aback by her bold offer. He knew she was over 18, just barely. He gave her a wink and a smile.

"No. Tonight I'm watching the football game and hitting the sack early. Busy day tomorrow. Goodnight, Naomi."

He hoped he saved her from embarrassment, but figured he really wouldn't know if he did until the next time he came in.

When home, Nick turned on the football game, but couldn't concentrate. It was getting late when he sent the text to Grace.

Is he still there?

He just left.

Do you want to talk? He offered.

There was a pause, then her response. *I wouldn't be very good company.*

Nick slipped on his jacket and gloves in record time and hopped onto his Harley. As he put on his helmet, he wondered if Grace had been crying. If that bastard did anything to hurt her…then he tried to stop that thought. He had this inexplicable urge to pummel Michael Dean and he'd only met him once.

He nearly flew across town and parked the bike in Grace's driveway behind her Land Rover. When he knocked on the door, he stood and waited. Grace opened the door in the dark.

"Come in, Nick…" she whispered.

The first thing he noticed as he snapped on the light was the tissue she had in her hand and how puffy her eyes were.

"Hey, what happened?" Nick was at her side within seconds.

Grace threw her arms around his neck. "I'm sorry."

"What're you sorry about? What the hell happened?"

"I wish I would have listened to you. Michael…he…"

She stammered and then stopped talking. Nick could feel her heaving as she sobbed against his chest.

"What did he do to you? What did he say to you?"

A fury began to build inside of him, but he remained steady.

"I'm scared, Nick. I never should've let him in." Grace wept uncontrollably.

"It's okay to be frightened. That's your instinct kicking in. Pay attention to that bad feeling." Nick tried to reassure her.

In silence, he moved Grace toward her sofa and she sat in the dark. Nick turned on the lamp next to the sofa. When he sat next to her, the glow made her face appear child-like, innocent. Even though she was two years older than him, she could pass for much younger.

"Let me get you a drink. You're shaking, Grace."

Nick wanted her to talk.

"Okay. Water, it's in the fridge." She spoke softly.

Nick moved to the kitchen. As he retrieved two bottles of water, he thought he caught the smell of Michael Dean's expensive cologne. *He was there in the kitchen with her. What did he say? More importantly, what did Grace say?*

As he handed her the bottle, she gazed up at him. "Thanks."

"I haven't done anything." Nick held her gaze.

"Yes, you have. Just being here like this. You've made me feel better."

"Do you want to talk about it?" Nick tried again.

He removed his leather jacket and tossed it onto the chair next to the sofa. As he sat next to Grace, his arm encircled her. He wanted so much to comfort her, relieve her anxiety. *Or, were these tears of sadness? Was she in love with this married guy and Nick was just a good friend? Was the night in the cabin her way of trying to peel herself away from Michael Dean?*

Although he wanted to know the answer to every question, he realized Grace was the type of person who would only let him in when she felt ready. His lips grazed her thick caramel-colored hair and he breathed in her scent. *If she only knew how much he wanted her. If she only knew how much he already loved her.* He never felt so defenseless in his life. Grace held his heart in her hands and she didn't even realize it. She could crush him with one sentence, one word.

* * *

Nick's strong arm felt so comforting, Grace wanted to feel sheltered like that forever. But, forever might not be in the cards if she told Nick everything about her relationship with Michael. In fact, she sheepishly declined to talk about Michael Dean. She sensed Nick's eagerness to get into a conversation about her past fling, but truthfully Grace was ashamed to tell him. The whole affair made her feel dirty, worthless, and humiliated. It might change Nick's opinion of her entirely. She couldn't take that chance.

"Grace, let me make you something to eat. You haven't eaten anything since earlier today, have you?" She felt Nick observing her closely. "You must be starving."

He was so patient and sweet with her. Grace took a long drink of water, then exhaled as she sat next to him. She loved the warmth of Nick's arm around her and she drew closer to him. For a while she curled up on his chest and pressed her face against his soft cotton sweatshirt.

"I'm listening to your heart beat." Grace whispered.

Then she spoke, trying to give Nick the information he seemed to want.

"I wish I'd never let him in. I told him it was over. I was going to say I've met a guy and I don't want anything to do with you, Michael. As I stood in front of him, I felt timid, weak. But I got my point across. Then, he kept pleading with me. He started crying. I told him to leave. I can't do this right now. It's too painful."

Her eyelids were heavy as she cuddled beneath a warm cashmere blanket Nick pulled over her.

For the first time in eight months, Grace had felt the old weakness for Michael creep in. She hated the feeling. She didn't want to impose on Nick, but felt herself clinging to him with the thought of never letting go. She had to pull herself together. She was on shift tomorrow night. She knew Nick would be working, too. *Life would go on.* Michael Dean would eventually go away, if she could remain strong. But, the thought of Michael coming back haunted her. How long would he persist?

Grace couldn't remember falling asleep, but when she woke in the morning she had a pillow beneath her head and was wrapped in the cashmere blanket, her favorite one. Nick was in the kitchen frying eggs and bacon.

"Hey sunshine – want some breakfast?"

* * *

Nick had been staring at her for an hour while listening to the radio. The cream color of the cashmere contrasted with her beautiful hair. Last night his hand stroked her head gently as she'd fallen asleep in his lap from exhaustion. He couldn't leave her. He slept on the sofa with his feet propped up on the coffee table. Even though his back was killing him, inside he had this overwhelming urge to guard her.

It was Saturday. A dreary dark autumn sky threatened rain. Paul's rehearsal dinner was planned for 11 AM. Nick tried to think of a way to bring it up without pressuring Grace. She may have made other plans for the day.

How could this Michael Dean mess with her head like this? Nick couldn't wrap his brain around it. In his world, no meant no. With all the willing babes out there who'd screw his brains out, why was Michael Dean pressuring Grace after she'd already broken it off with him eight months ago? There was no logic. He wondered if Dean held some sort of power over Grace. He knew from his training at the academy, domestic violence often played out this way. It was an act of pure possession, not of love or even sex. Only a sick bastard would continue to push himself onto a woman this way.

And, this sick bastard wanted Grace. Nick fantasized about bashing Michael Dean's perfect face into the ground with his bare hands. But, eventually rational thought reined in his savage contemplation. No. There would be other ways to deal with this. Tonight, he'd be back on shift. He wouldn't do anything foolish. He would wait for Dean to do that.

Nick put a plate with bacon and eggs in front of her. Then made her favorite tea.

"Thank you, Nick." Her eyes lingered with his and he felt himself melting. "I can't believe I fell asleep like that. I'm so sorry."

"Don't be. I loved every minute of it." Nick smiled. Even waking in the morning, she was beautiful.

"This breakfast is delicious. I'm starving." Grace pushed her hair aside. "Oh, I must look awful. I've got to take a shower." Before she left the kitchen, she gave him a peck on the cheek and squeezed his arm.

He stood at the kitchen sink and rinsed the dishes. As he stacked them into the dishwasher, he listened to the sounds of her showering and primping. He remembered the night in the cabin, replayed every detail over again in his mind. He could think of nothing except making love to Grace. The obsession seeped into every thought he had in his mind.

Grace padded into the kitchen.

"Oh, you didn't have to clean up, too. Wow, thanks!" She gushed.

Nick sat at the kitchen table.

"What are your plans for the day?" He tossed it out there.

"Shopping for food, getting my hair colored at the spa. Then, work tonight."

She gave him a little smile. That was a good sign. Then she added, "How about you?"

"Paul's rehearsal should be finished up by 2 PM. That'll give me some time before I go onto my shift at 3 PM."

Her face turned to the window. "A wedding rehearsal is such a beautiful thing, on such a gloomy day."

Nick watched as she gazed through the kitchen window.

"Gets dark early now. But, soon we'll gain more daylight once winter's solstice comes." Nick thought he sounded completely daft. He was trying to assess her mood and detected a somber tone.

"Nick, can I ask you a question?" Grace was now looking directly at him.

"Sure."

"Those girls, at your sister's wake yesterday…you know, the ones who were talking with you. Are you *involved* with any of them?"

"Wow – that came out of the blue. Why do you ask?" Nick almost choked on the words as he drank the last of his coffee.

"The way they *looked* at you, and the interaction you had with them ~ I was just wondering, that's all."

Nick felt like he'd better tiptoe through this subject. He didn't want Grace to know all his dirty little secrets; it might alter her perfect vision of him.

"They're friends, and yes, I've given them a ride home if they've had too much to drink. But none of them are my steady girl, if that's what you're asking." Nick hoped that would cover it without going into too much detail.

"Have you dated any of them? They like you. I'm sure you've noticed. Even the waitress at Bud's almost falls over herself to get you seated at your usual table."

"Damn, you don't miss much, do you?" Nick laughed, but it sounded hollow. She was very observant, maybe *too* perceptive. He had to be truthful. "Okay, yes, I've casually dated two of them. But nothing special. Not like with you…"

"You know what?" Grace put her cup in the dishwasher.

"What…" Nick felt like he might be taking the bait as she cast the line.

"When I first came here and worked at Cherryfield General, I remember you bringing in injured people. I even stopped and stared a few times myself."

Nick exhaled and smiled. "Yeah?" He knew it was a dopey smile, but he was so relieved to know Grace was one of his fans. "That's good. I'm glad you stopped and stared. So, you liked what you saw?"

Grace giggled. "Yes. You *know* I did. I still think about that night at the cabin. But you're so much more than a good-looking guy – you're my blue knight."

"Okay." Nick laughed. "I'll take that as some sort of compliment."

"Yes, it is." Grace turned and faced him. He noticed her beautiful pale blue eyes lowered. Her dark lashes contrasted against her ivory skin. How did it happen that a beauty like Grace saw something special in him? He didn't want to question it. He figured it would be better to thank heaven for the miracle.

As he moved closer, she placed her hand on his chest.

"Cherryfield Police Department," she whispered as her fingers touched the blue letters stitched on his sweatshirt.

"Yeah, they give 'em to us." Nick smiled as his eyes took in the details of her lovely face. "Would you like one?"

Surprising him, she placed her face against his chest once again and his arms instinctively drew her closer.

"Yes, I want *this* one." She whispered.

"Really? It's dirty, I've worn it for a couple of days...it's a size 2X..." Nick stammered.

"That's okay. I want it."

Nick stripped off the sweatshirt and wrapped her in it. Her cheek pressed against his bare chest and her hand traced his eagle tattoo.

"I love this, too." She sighed.

He couldn't stop the urge to bury his face in her hair.

"I love this, too." He exhaled into her ear, sure she felt the reaction she was having on him.

On a gray overcast day, as the rain started pelting the roof, Nick removed Grace's bathrobe and lifted her atop the kitchen island. Her lips were warm, sweet and willing. His hands slid across her silken skin and paused at her breasts. As he kissed her lips recklessly, a wild surge of excitement ran through him.

Oh yes, she wanted him. His lips brushed against her nipples and he felt her breathing become shallow. Once she even gasped. Her fingers moved through his hair, as he suckled her breast gently. Meanwhile, his hands skimmed the soft curve of her hips. As his hand traced the inside of her thigh, she guided him to the soft, wet place between her legs and Grace sighed with longing as he touched her there. He knew what she wanted and was more than happy to oblige. *Morning sex: if there was a more pleasing way to start the day, he hadn't discovered it yet.*

As she succumbed to his expert touch, her eagerness grew to explosive proportions. Her breath was uneven and with her hand guiding his, she exhaled a long shuddering sigh. Nick's jeans were suddenly too tight. He unbuttoned and they slid to the floor. Grace observed him from half-closed eyes. His hands and lips continued exploring her body and he knew what she wanted; it was growing exponentially between his legs. He drew a chair to the counter and sat. Grace's fingers were in his hair, moving him closer. As he moved his face between her legs and tasted her, she inhaled sharply and whispered, "Yes, yes."

Savoring the sensuous kiss, Nick felt waves of pleasure engulfing her -- once, twice, three times. Sensing she was ready, he finally stood and began to enter her. He eased his firmness against her gently at first. When he pushed inside, she cried out with a gasp of pleasure. Desire coursed through him as he thrust, slowly and deliberately at first. Her hips rose to meet him as she quivered with expectation. Then he moved together with her, harder, faster, deeper, until they reached a breathtaking shuddering ecstasy.

Panting and heaving, with his jeans around his ankles, Nick helped Grace off the kitchen island and held her in his arms for a long moment.

As he caught his breath, he whispered in her ear.

"Wow. That was incredible. *You're* incredible."

His mouth moved to the ticklish spot beneath her ear and he kissed her there.

"When can I see you again? Grace, I love you."

He hadn't planned to say that, but it was the truth and he couldn't repress it any longer. He waited for her reaction, hoping she'd say the same thing to him.

"Oh, Nick, you're so…wonderful." Grace kissed him and he felt as if he was drunk on love at that moment.

As Grace pulled her bathrobe around her, Nick zipped up his pants. He'd never made love to a woman like this. Yes, it was love for him. He knew it was because he had never felt this way with anyone else. He only hoped Grace felt the same. Maybe it would take her longer to say the words he wanted to hear. He was willing to wait as long as it would take. Unable to stop himself, he scooped Grace into his arms.

"Tomorrow, Sunday, Paul's wedding is at 11 AM. Don't forget, you're my plus-one."

"Oh, I haven't forgotten. I even found a new dress to wear. Come on, I'll show it to you."

Grace took his hand and led him into her bedroom. His eyes roamed over the antique white furnishings and marveled at how everything in the room reflected her. She opened the closet door and pulled out a soft pink dress.

"What do you think?"

"It's beautiful, but you wearing it will make it even more so." Nick smiled. It was the truth. She looked gorgeous right now in a flannel bathrobe.

Nick enjoyed her dimples when she smiled and how her eyes lit up when they met his.

"I don't get a chance to wear things like this very often. I'm usually dressed in scrubs or a doctor's smock. It's fun to be feminine and sexy once in a while."

He watched her put the dress back into the closet. When she turned he was close and reached his arm out and pulled her to him.

"Yes, it is fun, Grace. But when I'm with you, when we make love – it's a lot more than just fun for me. You know I have feelings for you. I can't help it. I'm in love with you." He waited and hoped she'd share her feelings with him.

She did, in a way. Grace's arms encircled his waist and she kissed him passionately.

"You're wonderful, Nick. I'm just afraid to get hurt again."

"I'll never hurt you."

"*He* said that, too." Grace pulled away. "I'm sorry I said that."

Nick pulled her back into his strong embrace. "I'm not *him*."

She buried her face into his chest. "I know."

"Give me a chance, Grace. That's all I ask."

Chapter 14

Paco had a long night riddled with hallucinations, nightmares, and more leg pain than he could tolerate. Thank God, Trish had arrived when she did. The lesser dosage helped take the edge off. She helped him through the worst night of his life. Even being on the battlefield and getting shot wasn't as grueling as kicking methadone.

"I think you're making progress." Trish said, sounding like an expert.

"Damn. I hope so." Paco responded as he soaked in a tub filled with hot water.

She was cooking on his tiny apartment sized stove, and, man this chick could cook. He could smell the bacon and knew she was making BLT's, one of his favorites. He just hoped the nausea had passed. But, he wasn't sure just yet if it had completely. The medical marijuana she had given him helped alleviate the leg pain, somewhat. At least he could stand up and walk a little. And, it helped with the nausea.

"Hey, look who's here – it's Nick." Trish was peering through the window. She opened the door and Nick slipped inside.

"How's things?" Paco heard Nick speaking in a muted voice with Trish.

"He's doing great. This is a long process…gotta hang in there."

Paco hoped she was right. He had reached the breaking point last night. The sweating was unbearable and the tremors awful. But, miraculously, today the diarrhea had stopped. Maybe she knew.

Paco got out of the tub and toweled off. He put on the comfortable scrubs Trish had brought for him from the hospital. They were soft and warm.

Nick slapped him on the back when he came into the kitchen.

"I'm proud of you, man."

Paco gave him a smile, although it hurt to smile at the moment.

"I'll get there. She's been a great help to me. Thank you."

Nick sat on the sofa as Paco finished the meal Trish had made.

As she cleaned the kitchen, Trish explained the schedule for the next few days.

"I've got to leave you for a little while, Paco, but a friend of mine – named Susan – will come by and make dinner for you tonight and hang out here for a while. I'll feed Diesel and walk him before I leave."

Trish moved through the door with a happy dog in his harness.

"I can't thank you enough for this, Nick." Paco spoke between bites. "Trish really knows how to cook bacon so it's crispy but not overdone. My taste buds have come alive."

"You don't need to thank me. Just pay it forward someday." Nick smiled.

"No. Seriously, man. No one ever gave a shit about me. Not my wife, or the friggin' VA…I mean, *no one*. I need to help you out. I'll get some more information for you. There's been trafficking around here – lots of it. Once I'm able to stand and walk outside, I'll get you plenty of photos. Especially that bastard who sold your sister that heroin."

"Don't push yourself too much right now. You're keeping this storage business going. Meanwhile, you're waging a war inside your body. I want you to win that war."

Paco felt Nick's hand on his shoulder. "Hey, I've got to go to Paul's wedding rehearsal. Stay safe, brother."

Paco watched as his friend drove away. Nick looked happy this morning. There was something different about him, a brightness in his eyes. He hoped Grace finally realized what a great guy he was. That was one way he could help Nick. He'd talk with Grace. He made a mental note to do just that the next time he had the opportunity.

Paco had always had a beef with law enforcement guys. He hadn't told Nick about that. The police were his enemy for the past year. But, the day Nick handed him a twenty-dollar bill it changed his way of thinking. Maybe these guys were human. Maybe a good many of them were like Nick. They'd come up the hard way and wanted to make the world a better place. Spending time with Nick, talking with him, Paco had a bird's eye view of what policing was really about. It was worse than being a soldier. At least, as a soldier, you were justified if you shot someone who was trying to kill you. As a police officer, Nick was scrutinized to the point of absurdity. Even when he was right, he had to prove it with dash cams and now a camera worn on his lapel.

Paco didn't know how Nick did it. The man had an unlimited amount of patience. He remained cool under pressure. He cared about the downtrodden, more than anyone would ever know. He was a quiet sort of guy, not the braggadocio type he'd imagined. The words Paco would use to describe Nick would be humble, truthful, kind.

A police officer was the last person Paco imagined he'd befriend. Another addict, maybe, or another homeless veteran, a stray dog, yes. A law enforcement guy – it was always out of the question. *Nick Kozlovsky had changed all of that.* And, Paco didn't have an easy mind to change.

At this point, Paco didn't want to let Nick down. He felt an obligation to get clean if he could survive it, and live a decent life. Because of Nick, he had a roof over his head and a job. Because of Nick, he had Diesel with him, healthy and strong. It wasn't that he felt he owed Nick. It was more than that. He wanted Nick's respect and friendship. Nick filled Paco with positive energy every time he came around. Even Diesel loved him. As the thought of Diesel occurred to him, the door opened and Trish presented Paco's dog back to him, fully exercised, tail wagging.

"I've got to go. But, I'll be back. Stay strong, Paco." Trish said as she hugged him.

She exited and Paco sat on the small sofa. He turned on the television for the first time in days. Diesel leaned against him. All was right with the world for a little while. The pain was waxing and waning, but wasn't constant now. Susan would stop by later on. The one person Paco missed was Tammy.

* * *

The rain continued non-stop, as Nick patrolled his sector on a black November night. *Saturday Nights*. He'd grown to hate them. Even normal citizens without substance abuse problems got into trouble on Saturday after dark. It was always the busiest night on his beat. After chasing two robbery suspects, and breaking up a fight in

Bubba's parking lot, he swung by the diner for a take-out salad with dressing on the side. He was determined to give up fast food, fast women, and feeling like he wasn't good enough. *There had to be more to life than just throwing himself into his work one hundred percent.* He fought against a wave of unlawfulness night after night, and fell asleep exhausted afterward. A good shift was not getting shot or beaten. It would be so wonderful to have a woman like Grace to come home to, someone who really understood what it was that made him do this thing. He knew few women could.

The radio crackled with a request from dispatch.

"Unit 12, please stop by the station. The Chief would like to ride with you for a while."

"10-4." Nick spoke into the microphone and put it back into the clip. Huh, wonder what's that's all about. The chief had never been in his cruiser on the night shift ~ ever. Nick did as he was instructed and pulled in front of the station. Chief Mackworth got into the front seat and clicked the seatbelt.

"Just drive, Nick. I want to talk with you, privately." Mackworth muttered. No eye contact.

Nick continued driving and sensed a shit storm was coming.

"The guy you apprehended, you know, when the cruiser window got broken…" Mackworth spoke deliberately. "He's pressing charges. He's got a lawyer, and claims you used excessive force in taking him down. He's got a broken rib, and some other bruises. He's also charging you with hate speech, he says you called him the N-word. We've got to address this, Nick."

For a moment, Nick couldn't believe his ears. The chief had always been a pretty good guy in his eyes. *But, what the hell was this?* Nick buried the anger burning in his brain and calmly spoke.

"I didn't use excessive force, sir. And, that racial slur isn't even in my vocabulary, never has been. He was running and I grabbed him. He tripped. I fell on him. I'm not exactly small, in case you hadn't noticed. I cuffed him quickly and pulled him to his feet because I was being surrounded by a crowd throwing heavy objects at me, putting not only my life in danger, but that of the guy in cuffs. And, just for the record, there were *racial slurs hurled at me*, but I didn't respond."

"I just want you to know you're being brought up on charges. I'm not here to be judge and jury. I am your superior officer. I believe you, Nick. It's just that this is going to become a media circus and I didn't want you to be caught off guard, that's all. We need to meet with the city attorney and go over everything, step by step. I don't want this asshole to win, either. But, we still have to go through the legal system. He has rights. But, you have rights, too." Chief Mackworth exhaled, as if exasperated.

Nick felt a headache coming on. "I'll do whatever I've got to do, Chief. But you should know these folks called me names. Racial slurs. I was having rocks and bottles thrown at my head. I moved quickly to avoid harm."

"We've got images from your dash cam, and we subpoenaed your lapel cam footage. I've already reviewed it. There's no evidence that you used excessive force, in my opinion. But, we don't know how this will play out. There are witnesses who say otherwise. It's going to be a long involved process. I just wanted you to be aware of it. You can drop me off at the station, Nick. I'm sorry to have to tell you all of this. And, I'm sorry about your sister. You doing okay?"

"Yeah. I'm coping." Nick exhaled.

"Tonight's your last shift until this investigation is complete. I'm sorry, Nick. You're a good cop. You'll be paid while the trial gets underway. Then, once the verdict comes down, if it doesn't go our way, our attorney will let us know if he thinks we can appeal. It's standard procedure. You're not the first cop this has happened to, believe me. It's becoming all too common and the cost to the city is enormous."

Nick's mouth felt dry as he dropped Chief Mackworth back at the station. He stood and saluted him. As he got back into his cruiser, Nick wondered about the incident. He couldn't recall doing anything that wasn't justified. But, an investigation would ensue and he'd be at the center of it, just because one guy accused him of something that wasn't even true.

"Unit 12 domestic at 42 Gray Street, shots fired."

Nick floored it with lights flashing, siren blazing. He spoke into the microphone.

"Unit 12 requesting back-up – 42 Gray Street."

As he approached the house, the lights were on but there was no movement. He parked his cruiser across the street and waited for one minute to assess the situation. He turned his siren off, but left the lights flashing. In sixty seconds, his eyes roamed over the scene he'd rolled up on. In the driveway, he saw the figure of a man, holding a gun to the head of a woman – a young child was on the staircase in the dark, crying. The man was moving and yelling something to Nick. He slid out of the cruiser and grabbed his tactical shotgun and slipped his Glock 22 out of its holster. Then crouched behind the cruiser out of sight.

Nick yelled toward the man. "Drop the gun, right now."

He was now living every cop's worst nightmare. Nick relied on his training. He repeated the command.

"Drop it. We can talk, but you need to put the gun down on the ground - now."

The guy was shaking and yelling something incomprehensible. The woman was screaming. Nick hoped she could knock the gun out of his hand or at least escape, but she seemed paralyzed with fear.

Nick knew he had 15 rounds in the Glock, but it would be a challenge to hit a moving target in the darkness. And, it was the last thing he wanted to do. Disarming the guy was his first choice, but he was concerned about the woman's safety.

Where the hell was his back-up?

Officer Stevens flew down the road, lights flashing, and stopped in front of the house. The man with the gun pointed at the woman now aimed the gun directly at Officer Stevens as he opened his car door. Leaning on the hood of his cruiser, Nick sighted his weapon center mass and pulled the trigger. Two rounds flew into the man's chest as Nick's weapon discharged. The man's body hit the ground but his weapon shot one round into Steven's cruiser, then the gun skittered across the driveway.

Stevens' head spun toward Nick. "Jesus, that was close. Call a wagon."

Nick called the ambulance as Stevens ran to the man's side to render medical aid. The woman was screaming and fell into a heap in the driveway. Nick dashed through the house to clear it. No one else was inside. Neighbors from nearby houses began to filter out.

Nick knew immediately upon pulling the trigger, the man he hit was dead. He was an excellent shot on the firing range and in tactical training, and now it paid off. Although, he wasn't feeling too great about hitting his target this time. The child on the staircase was two, maybe three years old. Nick gently picked him up and brought him to the mother. She wailed and held the child. A sinking feeling overtook Nick as he knew what would happen next. He'd be pulled off duty as the shooting was investigated.

Stevens put his hand on his shoulder as if reading Nick's thoughts.

"You had no choice, he was going to kill me. Neither of us can finish our shift. I'll call for replacements. I've been through this before, Nick. It's routine. I know that doesn't make it any easier."

"Yup." Nick nodded.

He imagined this would be more red tape, more bullshit. But, this was part of policing; the ugly side that they train you for at the academy, but you hope you'll never need. As the ambulance arrived and several other officers, Nick gave his account of what happened. Stevens gave his account. Nick could no longer think normally. There was a ringing in his ears. He kept seeing the dark figure in the driveway now covered with a sheet. As he watched the law enforcement team process the scene, he felt as if his life was washing away before his eyes.

As he drove back to the station and parked his cruiser, mentally he entered a long, dark tunnel. This was one he might never escape. An overwhelming sadness settled over him. It was the first time he had taken another human being's life. *He didn't want to do it.* The whole thing happened so quickly. The moment the man aimed the gun at Stevens, it was like a switch flipped in his brain. The action was automatic. He wanted to know about the man he killed. Why was he aiming a gun at the female's head? What pushed him to that act? Was he mentally incompetent? Or, a good man who just got drunk and snapped. Questions. He had so many. Nothing made sense any longer. He had just killed someone's father, someone's brother, someone's son.

He worried about how this would play out in the news. His reputation as a good cop was all he had, and now he might be finished. In a fog, Nick walked into Chief Mackworth's office and laid his weapon and badge on his desk.

The chief was calm.

"Heard about it, Nick. We got replacements for you and Stevens until this is settled. You okay?"

"Yeah. I mean, no. I've never shot anyone before. I'm sorry, chief."

The chief handed him a wad of paperwork on a clipboard.

"You can start by filling this out. Then there'll be an interview by internal affairs and a determination by a judge. It's routine, Nick. It will take a few weeks, maybe longer. Don't beat yourself up too much. We all go through this shit. It's part of the job, and it's the most difficult part. You did what you had to do."

"Yeah, I know."

Nick spent an hour and a half filling out paperwork underneath fluorescent lighting at the station. It seemed he was in a bad dream and couldn't awaken. A few other patrolmen walked by and put their hand on his shoulder but said nothing.

A sign of solidarity. The adrenaline had come and gone and the usual fatigue followed. He was craving sleep more than anything else.

As he sat there at the station filling out forms, he imagined it could be a long time before he'd be back there working, *if ever*. The station was his only home, the force his only true family. The reality of it was, he could lose the only thing that kept him breathing forever. All his life, he'd prepared to protect and defend. Now he needed a lawyer to protect him from those he was defending. It seemed surreal. But, he knew it was all too real. He had never hated himself as much as he did at this moment. It seemed the harder he tried to be a good guy, the more shit rained down upon him. Maybe he wasn't cut out for this life, after all. *Maybe it was all one great big mistake – his life – his struggle to be a better man.*

Only one guy would really understand him right now. He had taken the lives of others, too. And, he never judged him harshly, just listened. Occasionally a glimmer of sarcasm flashed in his dark eyes, as if he already knew it, lived it, and was tortured by it, too. Paco would understand. He understood everything.

Another batch of paperwork was put in front of him.

Chapter 15

Using night vision goggles, Paco watched the drug transaction taking place at the motel across the street. This looked like a big one. He wanted to get closer to write down the license plate number and maybe even get a snapshot of a face. These guys were brazen. For the first time in several days, Paco slipped Diesel's harness on and took him for a midnight walk. But, after walking a hundred feet or so, Paco felt his legs wobble. Walking was much more difficult than he imagined it would be. As he positioned himself at the edge of the road close to the motel parking lot, he aimed the phone and snapped several photos of the gang. One guy had opened a cardboard box and his buyer was sampling the goods. As Paco took a few steps closer to the cluster of people near the edge of the motel building, his foot caught on something in the brush. He tripped and fell which caused Diesel to bark.

"Hey, what the hell was that?" one of the men turned in his direction.

Paco crawled into the thick brush beside the road and pulled Diesel closer to him. He curled into a ball in the darkness. His leg pain had increased dramatically, and he knew running would be out of the question. He had overestimated his strength. He wasn't ready to walk yet, not outside anyhow. He hoped they wouldn't see him. Tall weeds surrounded him.

The footsteps in the dirt were barely audible, but got louder and closer. When Paco turned and looked up, a gun was pointed straight at his head. The flash from the barrel made everything go white, then he felt incredible pain in his chest.

The next thing he heard was a voice speaking.

"Come on. He's dead. Get the hell out of here."

Paco felt the dog as he nuzzled him. The pain in his chest was intense, but he continued breathing, or at least he thought he was. He couldn't get off the ground. His vision was affected and there was a ringing in his ears.

Diesel got close to him and leaned against his body. The canine whined and licked his cheek. Paco felt the warmth of his fur and his canine breath on his face. He didn't know how long he rested there. Paco had lost all concept of time or space. He closed his eyes and took a shallow breath. Ah, the pain was so intense. The phone was still in his fingers and he opened one eye and stared at the illuminated rectangle for a moment. His thumb touched the keypad and dialed 911, but he couldn't speak when the operator came on. That was the last thing he remembered.

* * *

It was well past midnight by the time Nick finished his paperwork. He'd talked with internal affairs and his union representative. It was a huge waste of time, but procedure. And, he'd just have to live with the consequences of doing his job.

He never felt so much like blowing off steam. He needed to talk with someone who would understand what it felt like to shoot another human being and be tested like this. He thought about Paco and drove in back of the storage buildings. As he tapped on the door in the darkness, there was no answer. His attention was focused on the ambulance across the street down the road.

He dashed toward the flashing lights and grabbed one of the first responders.

"What the hell happened here?"

Nick had changed out of his uniform, but the ambulance team knew his face.

"A shooting, this is bad. He's barely hanging on. We couldn't find anything on the guy for identification."

Nick ran to the gurney being shoved into the back of the ambulance with a white sheet covering a body, but Nick recognized the face. Blood was trickling out of Paco's head and his eyes were closed. He heard Paco moaning something, but couldn't understand him. Nick's heart nearly beat out of his chest. *No. No. No.*

"Time is of the essence. We got a chopper coming." One of the guys on the ambulance crew spoke hurriedly. "Two bullets. One went straight through his head, and one is lodged in his chest. He won't make it if we take him to Cherryfield. He needs a trauma center. We've called a chopper to get him to West Haven. Don't know if he'll make it."

Nick felt raw emotion overtake him. Rage, grief, anger, horror – he couldn't imagine *who* would do this to Paco.

"Hey, do you know this guy?" one of the ambulance crew asked.

"Yes." Nick responded. "He's on methadone, weaning off it. Make sure that's in his medical record. They need to know that."

"Yes, sir. I'll make a note." The medic typed into a tablet, then looked up.

"Hey, is this his dog?"

Nick's eyes moved to Diesel. His tail wagged when he saw Nick.

"Yes. I'll take him."

Holding back his emotion, Nick took Diesel's harness in his hands.

"Let the hospital know, I'm his next of kin. He's a veteran."

Nick couldn't speak any longer, the words caught in his throat. He watched from a distance as the chopper kicked up all sorts of debris, then landed. Within a few minutes they'd taken Paco on board, and disappeared into the blackness. He brought Diesel into his Jeep and started the forty-minute drive to West Haven. *Oh God, let him live.*

Nick's mind flashed forward. Paul's wedding. He'd never make it. Hopeful that Paul was still awake, Nick tapped his phone number. When his sleepy voice answered, Nick apologized for the late hour.

"I'm sorry. Something's come up on the job here. Can you get Cooper to do the best man thing?" Nick winced.

"Yeah. I'll call him right now. You okay, buddy?" Paul sounded concerned.

"I'll be okay. There was a shooting. It's not a simple thing to explain."

"I understand." Paul murmured. "Don't apologize. You're a policeman. Shit happens. That's why I'm a fireman. Hey, take care, Nick. I'll be thinking of you."

One more call as he hurtled toward West Haven. Nick tapped Grace's phone number and she answered on the third ring.

"Nick, what's going on?"

"It's Paco. He's been shot. I'm heading to West Haven; they're taking him in a life flight. I won't make it to Paul's wedding."

"Oh my God, Nick ~ Paco? Who the hell would shoot him? He's harmless. I'll meet you there at West Haven." Grace sounded panic-stricken.

"I've got this, Grace…" but the phone went silent.

When he pulled into the hospital parking lot, he rubbed Diesel's ears and told him he'd be back in an hour. As if the dog understood him, Diesel didn't bark or make a sound. He curled up in a ball on the seat.

Inside the hospital was a flurry of activity, even at 1:30 AM. The large urban area surrounding the place kept it filled with victims of violence and accidents around the clock. Once Nick got to the head nurse in the ER, he explained he was Paco's next of kin. She briefed him on Paco's admission and directed him to the elevator. Paco was already being prepped for surgery.

On the fifth floor, Nick stopped at the window to inquire about Paco.

"I'm his brother." Nick said. The young woman at the window contacted a nurse who appeared beside Nick in a matter of minutes.

"He's critical. Don't know if he's going to make it. But, we have the best doctor in the state performing the operation. I just want you to know he's in good hands. This physician has saved many lives in the past few months. We're fortunate to have him. Once the surgery is finished, Doctor Dean will come out to speak with you. I've got to go." She vanished through a locked door.

Nick sat down, leaned forward and put his head in his hands. Doctor Michael Dean. Right. *Oh God, let him live.* Nick's eyes were fixated on the clock on the wall. It had a sweep second hand and he watched it make revolutions as he counted the minutes. An hour passed. People moved in and out of doors, spoke in hushed voices. Nick wondered what would happen if Paco was dead.

The nurse arrived again in the waiting room holding a plastic bag.

"These are his belongings. He's still in surgery. No word yet. But, if we move him, you can bring that to him. His phone is in there." The nurse disappeared again.

*His phone…*Nick reached into the bag and tapped the iPhone. The last few photos were taken a few minutes before the shooting. He e-mailed the photos to the detectives back at the station with a brief explanation. Then, he scrolled through the photos on the phone, mostly of Diesel, some of Nick with Diesel, and even a photo of Grace with Diesel. The photo of Grace had been taken at the shelter. Nick slipped the phone into his pocket. *Evidence.* They'd need it. He remembered Diesel out in the Jeep. He took the elevator down to the parking lot, picked up some dog biscuits at a small corner store and brought them to him. Nick buried his face into Diesel's fur for a moment. Then took him outside for a quick break and put him back into the Jeep.

Back in the waiting room, the second hour was coming to a close. Nick wondered what was going on in the surgical room. *What was Doctor Dean thinking right now? Did he know Paco was a veteran? Did he know this guy was an amazing human being, that his life meant something?*

The nurse reappeared. "Doctor Dean will be out to see you shortly."

She vanished again. Nick sat with his face in his hands, feeling the ache of exhaustion settle into his bones.

"Excuse me."

Nick's eyes looked up and the man who uttered the words stood before him, Doctor Michael Dean. He recognized the surprise in the man's eyes and wondered what he was thinking.

"You – you're Grace's police friend – right?"

"Yes, sir." Nick got on his feet and waited for the verdict.

At the moment Nick stood, Grace appeared next to him.

"What's the prognosis?" She had been crying, Nick could tell.

Doctor Dean glanced at her, but continued speaking to Nick.

"He's stable but moving into intensive care. I removed the bullet lodged in his abdomen. A centimeter to the left and it would've been a different story. The bullet that went straight through his head may have done some damage."

Doctor Dean sat down, Nick sat next to him. Grace remained standing and Nick felt her hands on his shoulders.

Doctor Dean pulled out a pad of paper and drew a quick sketch of a brain.

"A neuro-surgeon worked on his head wound as I removed the bullet lodged in his thoracic abdomen. This patient was somewhat lucky. The head wound was a low velocity shot 9mm bullet – straight in and it exited right here. Skull fragments were removed. He was hit in the right hemisphere. We won't know how extensive the damage will be for weeks. The right side of the brain is mainly in charge of spatial abilities, facial recognition and processing music. It performs some math, but only rough estimations and comparisons. It also helps humans comprehend visual imagery and helps to make sense of what we see. It plays a role in language, particularly in interpreting context."

Nick absorbed the words, but wanted to know more.

"He's going to live. You're saying he's going to make it, most likely. But you don't know what the overall damage will be?"

Doctor Dean's eyes met his.

"Tough call. I'd say he could have some brain damage, but only time will tell. The brain scan indicated minimal bleeding, which is a miracle. But, we won't know for some time. As for the bullet I removed, no vital organs were destroyed except for his gall bladder. The bullet lodged right there. It appears he was wearing some sort of flack vest, an old battered one. When we undressed him just before surgery, the anesthesiologist was a veteran. He said it was an old one from the Korean War era. Not bulletproof, just protects the body from shrapnel. It definitely slowed down the bullet."

The doctor sketched a thoracic spine with a series of circles as organs.

"Here's where I did my work. He doesn't have a gall bladder any longer. But that's not of great concern. At first, we thought the bullet was closer to his right pulmonary artery. But, he was lucky."

"Thank you, doctor." Grace murmured. "When can we see him?"

"He's in recovery. It might be another hour or longer."

Nick watched Doctor Dean's eyes sweep over Grace. Before, he'd wanted to punch the guy in the face. Now, he wanted to hug him, and he did. Dean's body stiffened with surprise as Nick stood and put his arms around him and patted him on the back.

"Thanks, doc. I know this wasn't easy." Nick spoke with genuine gratitude.

Doctor Dean stepped back and his eyes met Nick's as if seeing him for the first time.

"Ah, you don't know how much of this I see. Gunshot wounds, stabbings, people beaten with crowbars. Children dying in their own neighborhoods. Bands of roaming thugs getting away with it, time and time again. It's *senseless*. But, I don't need to tell *you* that, officer. You're out there fighting it daily. I don't know how the hell you do it."

Dean turned and disappeared into the locked surgical area. Nick noticed he'd moved past Grace without acknowledging her. Nick embraced Grace, as tears slid down her face.

"It's going to be all right." He reassured her, even though he wasn't sure of anything.

When they finally got to see Paco, he was in a tiny cubicle in intensive care, conscious but groggy. The good news was, he could speak.

"Diesel, where is he?" Those were Paco's first words, slurred but intelligible.

"I've got him. He's fine." Nick assured him.

Paco's eyes closed and he drifted off to sleep.

"I'll stay with him." Nick whispered to Grace. You might want to take Diesel out of my Jeep and walk him, maybe take him home with you."

"Yes. I will. Nick, are you going to be okay?" Grace touched his arm.

"Yeah. I'm off duty. There was a shooting earlier. They're investigating. You know, I've got to jump through the hoops. They took my shield."

"Oh, Nick. I'm so sorry." She touched his arm and took the keys he held out for the Jeep. "This is my duplicate key. Thanks, Grace. I'll see you soon."

As Nick listened to Grace exit the cubicle, his eyes returned to Paco. The sounds of beeping, whooshing and tapping filled the room and he was lulled to sleep in the chair, for how long he wasn't sure. The nurse woke him and moved him to the leather sofa in the small waiting room. He felt like he was trapped in a maze.

He had thought nothing could be worse than losing his job, but he was wrong. It could always get worse. He should've learned that lesson from his childhood. He silently prayed for Paco to make it. Overcome by exhaustion, Nick curled up and slept.

* * *

As she walked out of the West Haven Hospital, Grace felt her heart sink when Nick said he had shot a man and had his shield taken away. She knew how much it meant to him to be a defender of the innocent, and now he was being treated as if *he* was the criminal. But, it was the system. And, now it would be a waiting game. She tried to put herself in Nick's shoes. How would it feel if a patient sued her and she lost the ability to practice medicine? She'd be mortified. Even though she had malpractice insurance that ate up a large portion of her salary, she had never gone through anything like that and hoped she never would. She'd worked all her life to be a doctor. This was her dream since childhood.

Diesel welcomed her with a yelp when she let him out of the Jeep. She walked along the sidewalk as she watched the first fingers of sunlight peer over the horizon. She realized at that moment just how tired she was. She had to get home, get Diesel settled in, and sleep before her upcoming afternoon shift. Grace put Diesel into her Land Rover and headed for Cherryfield and her comfortable bed.

Diesel was happy to enter her small house and sniffed every inch of the place. Then she took him into the backyard for few moments and yawned while waiting for him. Back inside, she prepared herself for bed. She put some leftover steak onto a plate and smiled as Diesel nearly inhaled it. She gave him a bowl of water and left him in the kitchen. She listened to his slurping as she rolled over and got comfortable under the covers. Within seconds, she felt the canine as he leapt upon her bed. He made a few turns and curled into a ball and fell asleep against her back.

Grace was filled with gratitude that Michael Dean had saved Paco. He was a talented physician; no one would dispute that. She only hoped Paco would make it. She said two silent prayers as she drifted off to sleep ~ one for Paco and one for Nick.

Chapter 16

Michael Dean tossed and turned that night wondering how involved Grace was with Mister Wonderful, her cop friend. She seemed to be smitten with the guy. He noticed how she put her hands on his shoulders while he explained the prognosis for his friend. Maybe now she'd realize he was one of the good guys – not just some married creep who wanted her *and* his wife, too. *Although, now that he thought about it, that's exactly what he had been. It's just that Grace finally saw through him.*

When he arrived home, he noticed a voicemail was on his phone and it was from Jeanine. When he listened to it, the voice didn't even *sound* like her. She was all business as she explained the time and place they were to meet for the mediation – he preferred to call it a *negotiation*. He knew she wanted every asset he had and then some. Jeanine was one smart woman. Once she found out about his affair with Grace, she swung into action. Of course, he was unaware of her knowledge until she drained their joint bank accounts and every liquid asset. The funds had been frozen by a judge and he was assured the divorce would proceed in a timely manner.

As he began to drift off, exhausted from the late night of surgery, he saw Grace's lovely face in his mind. She wanted children, she had told him that several times. He already had four and didn't want more. He'd have to reverse his vasectomy, but that wasn't always successful. He imagined he could give in to her demands and give her *one,* if he was lucky. But, then he wondered if that would be enough?

Grace wanted a life filled with friends and family. He already had the family and many friends, some divorced and remarried. Then his mind wandered to his daughters and his son. If he divorced, he knew it would fracture his relationship with every one of them. When it came time for his children to have their own brood, how would they feel about visiting grandpa with a bride much younger and a sibling nearly the same age as their child? *Awkward.* Or, would they *ever* forgive him? He might not be able to rekindle a relationship with them.

The more he pondered, it became clear that *he* was the one who stood to lose the most. The question had now changed in his mind. It wasn't *if Grace wanted him any longer* -- he knew the answer to that. But, did he want a young wife who would complicate his life and change it? By the age of 45, did he want to have a young child, golf less, and work more due to financial pressure? Did he want to work past the age of 65? He'd be 65 by the time his imagined child entered college.

Then there was Jeanine. She was one in a million. Many of his friends and coworkers had told him that often. But he always wanted more. And, when he met Grace, she rekindled his sex drive like no other woman ever had. But, his wife was devoted to him and had been for 30 years. Yes, she was aging, but she was still beautiful even though she was 42 years old. Could she ever forgive him? Would their relationship ever be the same? Too many unanswered questions.

Michael Dean closed his eyes and fell into deep slumber. His last thought was that of the man he had operated on. He hoped he would make it. The 24 hours after surgery was always most critical.

* * *

Paco opened his eyelids and slowly took in his surroundings. A pretty nurse appeared at his side, her blonde hair pulled back in a ponytail, she smiled at him.

"Feeling sleepy?"

His throat felt sore and raspy, but he answered her.

"Yeah. Like a truck ran over me."

"I'm going to move you a little so you can take a sip of water." Her brown eyes met his.

He drank slowly at first, then realized how thirsty he was.

"How long have I been here?" Paco asked.

"Three days." The nurse answered. Paco noticed she gestured to someone beyond his field of vision. A rugged blue-eyed man stepped into the ICU cubicle.

"Hey. Don't try to do too much just yet." Paco stared at him. What a kind gentleman. The first words out of his mouth were filled with concern.

"How'd I get here? What happened?" Paco knew this guy was familiar, but couldn't remember his name. The big guy came closer. His pale blue eyes seemed filled with concern.

"We've got the bastards who did this to you. You snapped a photo with your phone and the detectives got right on it. They got them, Paco. Same ones that sold heroin to Sophia. Same ones who shot Tammy at the methadone clinic."

"Who is Sophia?" Paco felt silly asking the question.

The nurse intervened with the nice guy. She called him Nick. He could hear the nurse telling him it might take a while for him to recognize him. She kept saying *let him sleep*. He needs to rest a little longer. Paco did fall asleep. The next time he woke, he had a different nurse. She had short dark hair and fed him soup and crackers. She held up a mirror and explained his injuries. He wondered why he had gauze wrapped around his head like a mummy. She told him it was a gunshot wound. And, explained the abdominal surgery.

"It's a miracle you're alive." She'd said with a smile. "And, your friend is taking care of your dog."

"I have a dog?" Paco muttered.

"Don't worry. He's fine. Grace is taking good care of him."

"What's his name?"

"Diesel."

Paco thought for a moment. If only he could remember who Grace was, maybe he'd remember Diesel.

The guy named Nick came in again. He showed Paco a photo on his phone of Grace and Diesel. Then he showed him something he remembered -- Strictly Storage – a small home. Photos of the inside, yes, that was his kitchen, his bed.

Paco stared at Nick.

"You're the cop, the good guy who helped me that day. You were pumping gas. Grace, she's the lady at the shelter. Diesel, he's my dog. The last thing I remember was being really sick, in the bathtub, my legs hurt. Oh, I was sick to my stomach. Methadone. That's it. I stopped taking it."

Nick leaned in. "How are you feeling now?"

"Hungry." Paco looked into Nick's blue eyes. "Yeah, I remember you. Deep blue. Truth. That's you."

"Me?" Nick smiled.

"Yeah. Your eyes. That's how I remember you. I didn't know your name the first time we met at the gas station, but your eyes were deep blue and filled with truth."

* * *

Nick left the West Haven Hospital filled with hope. Paco was beginning to remember some things. That was a good sign. As he pulled into the driveway of his ramshackle apartment building, the landlord was standing on the back porch.

"Ah, just the man I need to see." Mr. Broomfield smiled. "Rent is overdue."

He didn't even give Nick a chance to open the door. Shame washed over Nick for a moment as he thought about what to do. There was only one alternative right now. He handed the keys to his apartment to Broomfield.

"I'll pay the rent up to today, but I'm moving out."

Broomfield looked surprised. "Really? Where will you go?"

Nick didn't give him much information, but handed him the cash.

"Something's come up. I've got to take care of it. I'm sorry about the short notice, but with rentals being in high demand, I'm sure you will find someone right away."

Nick collected his belongings, mostly clothing and a few boxes of paperwork, and tossed them into his Jeep. Within a few hours, he was putting his stuff into a Strictly Storage unit and ran into Mr. Wilson.

"How's Paco doing?" Wilson asked.

"Making progress, but it might be slow. I'll take over for him here, if it's all right with you." Nick waited.

"Great. You're welcome to it. How're things at the police department? Not working out for you?"

"I'm taking some paid time off. My sister passed away. Plus, I was involved in a shooting on the job. It's routine. I need to lay low for a while and be patient. Not always easy for me, the patient part." Nick smiled.

"I heard about your sister, Nick. And, I read about the shooting. I'm sorry about it all. You can stay here until Paco recovers – that's if he does – good Lord willing." Wilson was genuine in his condolences.

Nick felt a sigh of relief escape. His debt had hit an all-time high. Not paying rent, he'd be able to put every penny onto his credit card. He thought about selling the motorcycle, then dismissed the idea. He would do it if he had to.

Wilson showed him the computer system and how to process a customer. He slapped Nick on the back before he left.

"Don't give up, Nick. Things will get better. You're one of the good guys."

"Thanks." Nick was surprised by his warm support. He watched Wilson disappear in his Cadillac and sat on the bar stool in the kitchen. He tapped his phone and Grace answered.

"Hey. It's me. You can bring Diesel over here. I'm at Strictly Storage. I'll be here until Paco returns."

"I was just thinking about you. I'll be over in a little while. You okay?" Grace's voice was tinged with concern.

"I'm good." Nick murmured. "Just concerned about Paco right now."

"I'll see you as soon as I get out of work."

The call ended and Nick was alone. He never felt so despondent in his life. He couldn't stop the questions that ran through his mind as he stared out of the window at The Bermuda Triangle. Would he ever get his badge and gun back? Or, would the liars and charlatans win? Would Grace see Doctor Michael Dean as her knight now that he saved Paco? She was in love with him once. That much he knew. Could he ever forgive himself for pulling the trigger, killing a man he didn't even know? If he didn't stop thinking these negative things, he felt he might fall into a deep black hole and never crawl out.

Stay positive. What could he do that would be purely positive? What would help Paco the most? *Tammy.* He called Grace back.

"Hey, it's me again."

"Hi. Are you okay?" Grace asked.

"Yes. I need to know how Tammy is doing."

"I'm not supposed to give out medical information over the phone without the patient's consent."

"Walk in and hand her your phone." Nick spoke deliberately.

"Okay. Hold on."

Nick waited and Tammy's voice sounded cheery as always. "Hi, Nick?"

"Paco wanted to know how you're doing. He's recovering from gunshot wounds from the same bastards who shot you. Do you want me to tell him how you're doing? Can you give Grace, I mean, Doctor Robertson, permission to tell me?" Nick waited.

"Sure. How is Paco doing? I saw it on the news – not many details."

"He's alive and recovering, but it might be a long road for him. He needs something, someone, to boost his spirit right now. He is very fond of you, Tammy. He asks about you often."

"Well, you can tell him I'm still alive and kicking. I'm thankful for bulletproof glass. It shattered but protected me. I got hit with shards but moved quickly enough to avoid the worst of it. I'm getting discharged tomorrow, hopefully. Yeah, you can tell Paco that." Tammy sounded upbeat.

"Great. Thanks. I will."

Grace came back on the phone. "Ah, now I understand…you're a devious man!"

"You have no idea…" Nick laughed and hung up.

The sunset brought Nick's thoughts back to his patrol sector as he mentally walked through what he'd be doing right now, roll-call, talking to his brothers, checking his cruiser, getting ready for whatever he would encounter on the night shift. He stood in the darkness and watched the traffic move down Parkway. In an hour or so, Grace would stop by with Diesel.

Some books were piled on the table next to the sofa and Nick picked each one up. Classics. Steinbeck, Hemmingway, Wouk. Paco had been doing some reading. There were philosophy textbooks, too. He fingered a tattered scrapbook for a moment, then realized it might hold Paco's treasured memories. Curious, he put the book on the kitchen table and turned on the light above. Page after page revealed Paco's life in photographs with a few words scrawled beneath each one. His beautiful ex-wife, her little son, a dog. Paco had a motorcycle, a Harley, at one time. Photos of Afghanistan, friends he had lost. Many pictures with his service dogs, Rambo, Camo, Bam-Bam. An old photo of his mother, father, and a sister. He never mentioned them. Then he found the obituary notice for his mother and father. He lost them in an auto accident. His sister died of cancer before she was 40. Nick closed the album, feeling as if he had intruded into a life once lived.

Another album caught his eye. It was right there on the table. The cover was new, barely used. He opened it and flipped through the photos of Diesel. There was a photo of Nick in there with Diesel, and a photo of Grace at the shelter, and pictures of the place he was standing in ~ Paco's home. This man had suffered so much loss, Nick marveled that he could even push himself forward to live another day. It was obvious to him Paco viewed his glass half full. An, old cliché, yes ~ but through all the negative, Paco managed to see the positive, even if it was only a faint flicker on the horizon.

Truth was, Nick felt his own self-pity dissolve as he paged through Paco's life. He had so much to be thankful for, even though he wasn't a police officer right now, he was still getting a paycheck. He had his health. His past was rough, but he was thankful for the hard lessons; the pain he experienced made him the man he was today. It hardened him, prepared him for what he was to see on the job. Even though he didn't know if Grace loved him, he wasn't going to give up. He knew he loved her. And, for the first time in his life, he realized he was worthy of love.

He slipped into his wool jacket and gloves and walked along the edge of the road. The Cherryfield Methadone Clinic had been repaired and he observed the addicts arriving and leaving. He walked by the Stop 'N Shop and saw a cruiser there, arresting shoplifters. As he made the pass by Bubba's Strip Club, his eyes roamed over the parking lot. The scanning was a habit that would never stop, always looking for things that didn't belong. Bud's Diner was a beacon of light in the darkness. He didn't have enough money right now to pay for a meal. His bank account was nearly empty until his next paycheck would be deposited. He walked back to the little house at Strictly Storage and let himself inside. He looked into the cabinet and found some cereal. He needed to lose weight anyway.

He saw the lights of her Land Rover pull around to the back and Grace was tapping on the door within a few minutes. When he opened the door, she removed Diesel's harness and the dog ran to Nick, tail wagging.

"Hey, buddy…" Nick rubbed the canine's ears.

"He's happy to see you…" Grace whispered.

"Not as happy as I am to see you…" Nick's eyes met hers. She was cold from being outside, rubbing her hands together. Nick moved toward her and pulled her into a warm embrace.

"I'll warm you up." He whispered. His lips moved just below her ear and he kissed her neck gently. "I missed you."

"I missed you, too." Grace murmured. "More than you know."

"How about dinner at Bud's tonight?" Grace asked.

"Um. I'm just having cereal. Plus, I don't want to leave Diesel alone on his first night back here." Nick hoped she'd buy that story.

"Okay. I'm starving. I'll have cereal, too." Grace smiled.

Crunching together at the table, Grace talked about her busy day at the hospital. Her face was animated as she related a few funny stories in the midst of the gruesome things she witnessed. Nick imagined this was how it would be if he was with her. He'd come home and share his crazy stories and she'd give him her rendition of life in the emergency room. When she finished eating, she tucked her hair behind her ear, an endearing little gesture that made him ache for wanting her.

"Oh, I'm so tired. My feet are killing me." Grace exhaled.

"Here. Sit on the sofa, take off your shoes, let me handle this." Nick steered her gently.

He sat on a tattered footstool before her after finding a bottle of hand lotion in his duffle bag. Grace giggled as he took her foot between his big hands.

"I've never had anyone do this before. It tickles a little."

"Don't worry. I'll apply some pressure in the right places. You sit back and relax."

Nick felt the supple skin of her feet and kneaded expertly. Eventually, the tension began to leave her. Diesel hopped up on the sofa next to Grace and leaned against her.

"He wants you to pet him." Nick nodded.

He listened as Grace cooed to the dog. She was gentle and kind with all living things. Nick envisioned her as a mother. She'd be a good one. Efficient, but loving and sweet.

"What are you thinking about? You're so quiet." Grace turned her attention to him.

"You'd be surprised."

"What…oh, come on…tell me."

"I was thinking about what it would be like to be with you like *this*…on a daily basis. Okay, I was fantasizing about being married to you." He waited for her reaction.

"That's a nice thought, Nick." She smiled.

"Have you ever had thoughts like that?" Nick knew he was laying it on the line, but couldn't help himself. He had to know.

"Yes. I'll confess, officer. All my thoughts – right here, right now. I'm impressed with you in so many ways. How you've handled the last few days revealed your true character. I know it hasn't been easy, Nick ~ losing your badge, your gun, your identity as a police officer. You've been a great friend to Paco, given of yourself freely. You've been a wonderful, supportive shoulder for me. Whenever I need you, you're there. I've thought about how you've been a sentinel, watching over your family members all your life, and now, still watching over this city. I admire you, Nick, more than you know."

For a brief moment, Nick nearly stopped breathing. The things she said filled his heart with emotion, gratitude, and made him love her more, if that was possible.

"I thought there was an unresolved thing between you and Doctor Dean." Nick couldn't stop himself from uttering the words. He had to know.

"That's done. I've spent the last year of my life exorcising that demon from my soul. He's gone. He's a good doctor, yes. I appreciate the fact that he saved Paco. But, it's over between us. I reached that conclusion the night you came to my house and slept on the couch."

Chapter 17

Grace leaned forward and pulled Nick toward her. She could no longer deny the love she felt in her heart for this man at her feet. He was everything she needed, everything she wanted. She had to let him know. If she didn't, she was certain another woman would.

Her hands held Nick's face and his eyes fixed on hers.

The words escaped her lips in a breathless whisper. "I love you, Nick Kozlovsky."

It was as if an *on* button was pushed inside her body. It wasn't like her to make a move on a guy. But before Nick could speak, her lips were on his, and her kiss was slow and thoughtful.

On his knees before her, Nick's arms encircled her waist. His mouth hungrily devoured hers and she savored the warm wet sensation. His kiss sent tingles through her entire body. Surprising her, he stopped for a moment, his pale blue eyes danced with hers.

"I love you, Grace Robertson." He exhaled.

Grace's hands moved to the back of his head and stroked his hair. She kissed his forehead, his nose, his cheek. His lips were on hers again, his tongue probed and she let him in. His open mouth was sweet, tender, inviting. The feeling of his tongue dancing with hers took her breath away. She unbuttoned his shirt and her fingers explored his powerful chest. She felt herself losing control. It was a delicious feeling ~ reckless, wild abandoned pleasure. Her hands moved over his abdomen and she sensed his response. She was breathing against his ear as he planted warm kisses on her throat. Her shirt was open. His lips traced kisses down to her breast, and she waited excitedly for his mouth to take her nipple.

Oh yes. Nick knew how to make love to every inch of her body, methodically, slowly, sensually building her to a fever pitch. Every minute with him was enjoyable. As his hand caressed her thighs, she parted her legs. His lips were on her mouth once again, his kiss urgent, eager. His thumb moved rhythmically over the sweet warmth between her legs until she throbbed and cried out.

As she climaxed, his mouth covered hers and he kissed her like she had never experienced before. In a heap, in his arms, Grace tried to catch her breath. For a moment Nick held her, as her heart hammered with passion.

Still breathing heavily, she felt Nick's strong arms lift her and he placed her gently atop Paco's bed.

"Yeah, I changed the sheets a little while ago and cleaned the bathroom, too." He smiled as he removed his pants and reclined on the bed alongside her.

Grace cuddled against his upper body. How she relished the warmth of his chest, the private enjoyment as she traced her finger over his skin. She pressed her cheek against his body and listened to his beating heart. This was what she wanted, forever. There were no doubts. She felt his hand in her hair. Her fingers drifted over his abdomen, then down to the patch of hair below, and she heard him inhale sharply. Moving her body above him, she kissed the eagle tattoo. The masculine scent of his skin made her ache for him. Placing light kisses beneath his naval, she took the hard flesh in her hand and heard him respond with delight. Her lips took him in and her tongue caressed the soft smooth skin. As she continued exploring his entire length with a slow and steady motion, she felt him move. With her hand at the base, she massaged the hot smooth flesh and watched him pulse with pleasure. She sat atop him and took him inside her. As she did, a wave of ecstasy overtook her. She heard Nick make a sound of excitement and shared the thrill with him.

After climaxing together, Grace moved to his side and his arm cradled her against his chest. "I've never felt like this." He whispered.

"Mmm you are beautiful." Grace said, content to look at his male form for hours. He didn't seem to be aware of the fact that he was a feast for her eyes.

"I don't want this day to end." Nick said as Grace cuddled closer.

"It doesn't have to." She whispered.

"You'd stay here, with me?" He seemed surprised. But, Grace had decided she would be with Nick through his trials and whatever else came. She wanted to comfort him and love him through the darkest hours. That's what real love felt like. True blue. Deep. Together as one.

"Yes. I'll even cook you breakfast in the morning." Grace murmured. The smile of satisfaction on his face said everything she needed to know.

Cee-Cee was right. He had been standing right in front of her for the past eight months, disguised as a blue knight. She just hadn't noticed him. She was too wrapped up in the pain of the past to see the possibility of the future. Real happiness had been right there before her eyes.

* * *

For the next two months, Nick fell into a routine he didn't want to end. He had imagined this would be the lowest moment of his life, but just the opposite occurred. Every night at sunset, he walked Diesel through The Bermuda Triangle, with a concealed .38 strapped beneath his jacket. His brothers in blue acknowledged him. They'd often stop at the side of the road and chat for a few minutes and fill him in on what was happening. The chief's request for more manpower had been squashed by the city's budget committee. *Do more with less.* Yeah, the same old thing.

If Grace was working the night shift, she'd come by in the morning and he'd cook eggs and bacon for her, or an omelet. She'd walk with him afterward and marvel at the crime taking place on a daily basis. Nick often sent a text to his brothers when he saw suspicious behavior taking place. Arrests were up. More criminals were being removed from the streets. This gave him a sense of accomplishment.

But the part of his day he enjoyed most was seeing Grace. If she worked the day shift, she'd arrive for dinner late in the afternoon. Nick would often make his special chopped salad with his secret dressing and grill chicken or steak. Then they'd go for a nighttime stroll with Diesel.

On snowy nights, they'd sit in Paco's small house and watch the news and make love. He relished those moments, lived for them, actually. Nick spent time at Grace's bungalow and helped her decorate for Christmas. When Grace found out he never had a home-cooked Christmas dinner, she insisted on making one just for him. A trip to the grocery store with Grace was a treat. She had a quirky sense of humor and made the most mundane things fun.

In fact, Nick had never experienced this depth of love. He loved Grace so much, he felt they were inseparable. He found himself texting her whenever they were apart. He left notes for her in the morning by the coffee pot. And, she would leave notes for him in his pants pocket or by his toothbrush. Making love became a daily ritual, something Nick savored morning or evening.

Even though he had little in the way of physical assets, he never felt so rich. He had never experienced the sheer delight he did each day with Grace in his life. And, Diesel brought him immeasurable joy. He became Nick's constant companion and traveled everywhere with him.

Three times a week, they'd visit Paco at the nearby veteran's rehab. He was making progress, but it was slow. They invited Tammy along to visit Paco. The two had a great time talking and promised to meet again. Nick brought Diesel in to see him, with permission. Paco's face lit up when he saw his buddy.

As for the balance on Nick's credit card, it had finally started to decrease. He knew if he sold the motorcycle, he could pay the rest of it off. But, he didn't want to do it just yet. He wanted to get through the legal battles ahead.

* * *

As for Grace, cooking Christmas dinner for Nick was a joyous occasion. She knew his childhood had been rough, but never realized how much he'd missed until now. Little by little, he told her what his life was like as a child. As Grace learned the details, her heart broke.

As he arrived at her house on Christmas Eve, she had an evening of traditional fun planned. More than ever, Grace wanted Nick to meet her family.

"Eggnog! Wow, this is the real thing." Nick sipped the concoction that Grace made every year for her sister and parents.

Dinner was almost ready. She wondered if Nick was nervous about meeting her parents and her sister. Grace watched the clock and heard the car drive in. As she opened the door, her parents entered and hugged her. Nick was at her side as he shook their hands and introduced himself. Grace's sister, Rachel, hugged Nick and her husband Ralph, shook his hand.

Nick seemed touched when Grace offered to say a prayer of thanks for the meal. He held her hand and closed his eyes. She sensed this was all foreign to him, as he was quiet most of the time unless her parents asked him a direct question.

"So, what do you do for work?" Grace's father began as he carved the turkey.

"Police officer." Nick answered.

"How do you like it? Have you been on the force long?"

"I love it. Four years, sir."

"On vacation?" Her father's question hung in the air for a moment.

"On paid leave." Nick answered.

"Well, that's great to get paid leave at Christmas." Grace's sister interjected.

Grace busied herself with drinks and serving everyone. She sensed that Nick could handle himself just fine. No need to rescue him.

After dessert and coffee, they opened gifts. Grace sat close to Nick on the sofa and couldn't stop herself from cuddling beneath his outstretched arm. She wondered what her family thought of Nick; they weren't easy to read. Father was a physician and mother was an administrator at a bank. Rachel and Ralph were employed in finance and lived in New York City.

When Grace's family kissed her goodbye at the door, Nick stood beside her. Rachel whispered in her ear as she hugged Grace. "He is delightful."

After the car drove away, Grace worked next to Nick in the kitchen loading the dishwasher. He was quiet for a few moments, then asked the burning question.

"What did she say?"

Grace stood in front of him at the kitchen island. "She said you're *delightful*."

"Really?" Nick's mouth curled into a smile.

"Yes." Grace couldn't stop herself. She wrapped her arms around his waist.

"I couldn't agree more."

His lips were on hers in an instant. She tasted gingerbread muffins and whipped cream.

"Remember the first time you stood here at this kitchen island with me?" Grace teased him. "That's something I will never forget."

"I remember every detail." Nick exhaled into her ear. "The bathrobe, how nervous you were, how beautiful you looked, everything."

Nick touched his chest pocket. My phone's ringing. Who'd call me on Christmas Eve? Grace watched his brow furrow as he answered. She heard him say, "Yes, sir. Okay Chief."

When he ended the call, he beamed. "Best Christmas present ever!"

"What? Oh, come on --- tell me!" Grace shook him.

"I'm back on the force as of January 1."

Grace's eyes filled with tears. It was as if her prayers were answered.

Chapter 18

Prior to Christmas, he had testified at his trial with the expert advice of a union representative and an attorney. After a short and public battle in the press, the charges were dropped regarding use of unnecessary force and he was found innocent on the charge of using racial slurs. In fact, the footage played at the trial showed just the opposite. Racial slurs along with heavy objects were being thrown at Nick but he kept his head.

The week after the shooting, he testified regarding the incident. He expected to wait longer for the decision, but the whole thing was recorded on two dash cams and his lapel cam. There was no doubt Nick's actions possibly saved Herrick's life and the life of the woman being held with the gun to her head.

The whole thing had been hanging over him like a black cloud. He wanted to be a better police officer, more sensitive to those in need. But it was difficult when you rolled up on someone threatening you or an innocent person with a firearm. That changed the whole dynamic immediately. He thought through the incident many times, and wondered what he could've done to change the outcome. But, he always came up with the same answer. The guy pointing the gun at Herrick made the threatening move, which forced Nick's decision.

With the worst behind him, Nick was looking forward to the first week of January.

In a massive snowstorm after Christmas, he made his way to the VA rehab to see Paco. Tammy was there when he arrived and he was happy to see her.

"Hey, how are you doing?" Nick asked Tammy.

"Much better. I'm working at Bud's Diner. The girls said that you haven't been around lately."

"No. I used to be a regular. I think cooking with Grace has taken up my time lately. And, that's a good thing. I've lost some weight." Nick patted his abdomen.

"I was just leaving. So, I'll let you guys talk." Tammy reached down to rub Diesel's ears. "He's so cute."

As soon as she left, Paco waved Nick closer.

"Hey, I asked her out on a date and she said yes!"

"Wow, that's great!" Nick placed his hand on Paco's shoulder.

Paco's face became serious. "So, when are you going to pop the question with Grace?"

Nick eyed him. "How'd you know I came here to talk about that?"

"It's high time you did *something*. Sit down. You need a little shove in the right direction, I think." Paco's eyes twinkled with mischief.

"Okay, I'm sitting. I'm prepared for your words of wisdom."

"Valentine's Day. You've gotta seal the deal with Grace. She's in love with you, Nick. You've gotta know that by now."

"Yeah. I know that. I've got *nothing*, Paco. Heck, I'm living at your place. I can't even afford a rent right now, let alone a ring. I want to do it properly. Grace deserves that."

"It's not about stuff. It's about *love*. That's all she cares about. Trust me. I've been around Grace enough to see how she looks at you. I've heard her talk about you. She is smitten, I'm telling you, brother. Don't let this chance pass you by. You're only going through this life one time, you've gotta grab the good stuff when you get the chance."

"Okay. Let me think about it. I need a plan. Valentine's Day. I need to do this on a tight budget, you know?"

"I've got ideas." Paco smiled and suddenly Nick had the feeling he had better listen. So far, everything this man told him was true. He trusted Paco's judgment.

For the next half hour, Paco described an inexpensive scenario for Nick to ask Grace to marry him. The more he listened, the better it sounded. By the time he left, he had a list of things to work on.

* * *

Grace was brushing her hair in her office listening to the weather report on the radio. Another snowy night in her bungalow with Nick was exactly what she was hoping for. He closed the storage place up at 5 PM and would be at her house right after that. The drive home was nerve-wracking, but she finally got to her driveway and found a pleasant surprise. There he was shoveling it. Nick, bundled up from head to toe, finished one of the jobs she most dreaded. She could get used to this.

"Hey, thanks!" She hugged him and felt his warm breath against her face.

"Time to go inside." He pulled her through the door.

After removing several layers and placing his wet clothing on the radiator in the entryway, Grace pulled him onto the sofa.

"I love having you here when I get home." She felt his lips take hers and was swept away with longing for him.

"I picked up a pizza so you wouldn't have to cook." Nick smiled.

"Oh, goodie." She kissed him again. "I didn't want to cook tonight."

"No? What did you have in mind?" His devilish grin made her pulse quicken.

"Oh, you know, what most people do on a cold, snowy night."

"Hmm. What's that?" His arms encircled her.

"Keep warm by the fire." Grace murmured. His lips were on her neck and he was unbuttoning her shirt.

"I need a shower. I just got out of work." Grace said between kisses.

"I can help you with that, too." Nick ushered her toward the bathroom.

As the hot water pulsed over them, Nick took her into his arms and nestled his face into her hair. "Oh, I have waited all my life to do this."

For the next hour, Grace forgot about dinner, she forgot about the snowstorm, she forgot what planet she was on. Nick made the shower her favorite place in the world. His mouth, his hands, his sense of timing was incredible. He knew exactly what she wanted and just how to deliver it.

She was wrapped in a big fluffy towel, then slipped into a warm soft robe. As the two of them shared a pizza in front of the fireplace, Grace wondered how she had lived without this for so long in her life.

* * *

Being back in The Bermuda Triangle, Nick patrolled his beat, connected with his brothers every night, and life started to take on the feeling of normalcy. That's if anything to do with policing could be considered *normal*. The bulk of his time was spent breaking up domestic disputes, hauling drunks to jail to sleep it off, and talking with the citizens of Cherryfield in order to forge a relationship with them. Grace made him want to be a better man. Paco made him want to be a better cop.

Every time he visited Paco, Nick noticed he had gained a little more weight and seemed to be improving. Paco's optimism became Nick's inspiration. He smiled every time he saw Nick walk through the door.

"I'm looking forward to February 14th. How about you?" Paco now laughed.

It was good to hear him laugh. No longer addicted to methadone, Paco was a success story in Nick's book. This was what drove Nick. Helping. Being kind. Lending a hand. Talking and listening.

Valentine's Day was fast approaching. He made his plan to take Grace out for a special dinner. He had a burning question to ask.

As it turned out, February 14th was the date of Paco's discharge. Nick was at the facility bright and early to drive him home. He looked good. Not only had he recovered from the ravages of addiction, his gunshot wounds had healed. Only scars remained, and Paco said they matched nicely with the others he had from Afghanistan. Nick pulled the Jeep up to the entrance of the rehab facility and Paco got in with no assistance.

"Hot damn! I'm a free man!" He howled as Nick drove away.

"You had some cute nurses in there." Nick teased him.

"None as cute as Tammy." Paco remarked.

When they rolled into the parking spot at Strictly Storage, Nick sensed Paco was having a moment. He opened the door and Diesel greeted him in the parking lot, tail wagging, and he made that funny whining and barking sound he always did when he saw Paco.

When Paco stepped inside, Nick noticed tears rolling down his face. Paco grabbed Nick and gave him a bear hug.

"Thanks, man. This place looks great. I appreciate everything…"

"Hey. No need to thank me. I spent a lot of time here…thinking."

"Good thoughts, I hope." Paco smiled.

"Yeah. Everything is ready. I'm going to ask Grace to marry me tonight."

"Everything's set up?" Paco pressed him.

"Yes. I don't have a ring yet. I looked at the pawn shop. I just can't afford a diamond right now. But, I've got to ask her. She's the one. You were right, Paco. There will never be another woman like Grace in my life. I need to do this now." Nick shared his deepest feelings.

"Wait a minute." Paco scurried into the bedroom and came out with a small wooden box in his hand. "I got something here. It's old, but hell, when I was using -- I almost sold it."

Paco laid a gold ring on the table. It was a round white diamond set into an elaborate floral design with tiny diamonds surrounding the big one. It was unique. Nick had never seen one like it.

"It's old." Paco stated. "I mean *really* old. It belonged to my grandmother, or maybe her grandmother. I'm not sure any longer. It's an antique. I know that much. Came from some fancy European designer a hundred years ago. The guy at the pawn shop told me to hold onto it. So, I did. When I was using, I hung onto it thinking I could use it if I had to score. But now you can use it to score with Grace. I want you to take this and give it to Grace for Valentine's Day. You *can't* propose, man, without a ring."

"Oh no, Paco. I can't take this. It's too precious. It's part of your family's heritage." Nick argued.

"You *are* my family."

The moment Paco uttered the words, Nick was deeply touched. He also knew Paco had his mind made up. And, once that happened, Nick knew it would be hard to change.

"Please, I insist." Paco looked him in the eye. "This is how I can help you. I want to see you happy, man. *Let me do this for you.*"

Nick had never heard those words before. The concept was alien to him. No one did things for him, *ever*. It was always the other way around. He paused for a moment and saw the tears in Paco's eyes. It meant so much to him. He understood Paco's need to give something back. That feeling of giving – it was the very thing that sustained Nick his whole life. He couldn't say no to Paco.

"Okay. I'll take the ring, but you've got to do one more favor for me." Nick spoke with authority.

"Sure. Anything." Paco said.

"Call Tammy and tell her you're home." Nick smiled.

Paco grinned and his dark eyes filled with mischief.

"You think she'd come here to see me?"

"Yes. If you invited her." Nick smiled. "I'll let you in on a little secret."

"What…" Paco was intrigued.

"She told me to call her when you got home." Nick whispered.

At that moment, Nick put the lottery ticket on the kitchen table in front of Paco.

"I found this in your belongings. You purchased it the first day I met you at the gas station. Remember that?"

"Yeah. I'll never forget that day."

"Well, you'd better check the number. I think you've got a winner. I'll drive you up to the lottery office tomorrow to collect it." Nick couldn't stop the smile beginning to take over his face.

"How much is it?" Paco's eyes grew wide with wonder.

"Well, Stop 'N Shop couldn't pay it. They said you'd have to go to the lottery office. They're holding it for you."

"Hot damn! This is my lucky day!"

Paco picked up his phone and brought up the lottery website. Nick watched as he scrolled through the dates and paused. For a minute, he stared at his phone and double-checked the number to make sure it matched.

"A hundred thousand." Paco whistled. "Wow!"

"What're you going to do with all of that?" Nick couldn't stop laughing. They were both giddy at the same moment. Nick had never heard Paco express joy like that.

After a few minutes, a contemplative expression settled upon Paco's face. Nick wondered what was going on in that mind of his. When Paco's eyes connected with his, he was deadly serious.

"I don't need much. I mean, maybe ten thousand in a savings account. I want to give this to a veteran's group. I heard about them from a guy I met at the VA while I was rehabbing. Every dime goes directly to returning service dogs to their handlers. Not only do they bring the dogs back, they also build houses for homeless vets to live in."

Nick was speechless. Here was Paco, who was recovering from his war wounds, and gunshots taken from drug dealers, left for dead ~ yet, he wasn't thinking of his own welfare. It was all about his brothers and helping them.

Already, Nick had learned so much from Paco, but now appreciated the magnanimous nature of this man. Nick shook his hand.

"You're impressive, Paco. I've got to say. You never cease to amaze me."

"There are people, Nick ~ I know them. They're a lot worse off than I am. This makes me feel good, like I'm making some small contribution to help. You know, sort of like you do. You're a cop, yes. But it's a lot deeper than that. You're a good guy. You came up the hard way but you know the best things in life aren't things."

* * *

Grace wore the soft pink dress as she got ready for Valentine's Day. She never got to wear it for Paul's wedding. She excitedly swept her hair into a twist and dabbed on a little bit of make-up. As she moved into the kitchen to get a drink of water, she heard the key rattling in the lock and Nick appeared in the doorway. He wore the charcoal suit, the one she loved on him, but this time he added a bright red tie.

"Hey, handsome, are you taking me someplace special? I don't get asked to wear a dress very often." She teased him.

"Yes. It's special. I don't put this suit on very often either. It's usually a very sad occasion or a very happy one."

"I'll hope it's the latter. Where are we going?" Grace couldn't imagine what he had planned. She knew he was strapped for cash, but would never mention it.

"I don't want to tell you where we're going, it would ruin the surprise." Nick smiled. Now she was really curious. What surprise? It was Valentine's Day. Every restaurant in town would be booked. She wondered which one he chose for the reservation.

The temperature got up to 30 degrees that night, but the wind died down. Nick held Grace's long wool coat as she slipped into it and buttoned up. She wore gloves and got into the Land Rover and tossed the keys to Nick.

"You might want to drive. I plan to have a glass of Champagne tonight. Don't want to get picked up." She giggled.

Nick drove through Cherryfield and toward Bud's Diner. Oh, gosh, Grace wondered if this was going to be old home night at Bud's for a moment, but he drove by and turned at the storage facility. Grace saw the lights on and Nick stopped in the driveway.

He touched her hand. "Paco's home. I thought we should welcome him home."

"Oh, Nick, that's wonderful!" Grace was elated. The two of them shivered as they waited for Paco to open the door.

"Come in. Well, look at you two!" Paco acted surprised.

"Look at *you*!" Grace embraced him. "You look great, Paco. Welcome home! It must be wonderful to be home. Diesel must be so happy."

"Yeah. Well, don't let me hold you folks up. Looks like you're going out to dinner." Paco made eye contact with Nick. Grace wondered if something was up, but didn't say anything. They were close, that much she knew. It was probably some sort of man joke between them.

As they stepped back outside, she heard Paco's voice. "Have a great night."

As Grace moved toward the Land Rover, Nick took her by the hand.

"No. This way." He walked in the direction of the storage units. When he got to the one he had rented, he opened the door. She saw his motorcycle in the back but the rest of the storage unit was decked out like a first-class restaurant. White curtains hung around the space, there were tiny white lights and a table for two. Tom, one of Nick's friends stood by the table dressed in black. An iPod sat in the corner playing soft piano music.

Tom nodded to Nick. "Table for two?"

Nick smiled. "Yes, and the food better be good."

Grace giggled. They sat at the table and Tom lit the candles.

"Dinner will be served in 20 minutes. Here's your Champagne." Tom popped the cork and put the bottle into the ice bucket. Then he winked at Nick, nodded and left. A space heater kept the room warm and Grace watched in amazement as Nick poured her a tall glass of Champagne, and put a little bit in his glass.

"This is a special night, Grace. Do you like this? It's a private spot for the two of us."

She was nearly speechless. "Okay. It's beautiful. I'm shocked and amazed. You couldn't have done all of this on your own."

"No. The guys helped. Tom insisted on cooking. Paul decorated the place. Paco picked out the Champagne. But I selected the music." Nick smiled and had a little mischief in his eyes.

"Everything is beautiful. I love the music." Grace whispered.

"I need to dance with you, Grace." Nick clicked the remote for the iPod and a song came on.

She was swept away to the words of the song, *Thinking Out Loud*, and she had no idea Nick could dance. He was light on his feet and held her snugly against his core as he spun her around a few times and kissed her neck. When the song ended, Tom reappeared, this time with two plates. He placed them on the table and added a bottle of iced water and disappeared.

"Wow, talk about taking my breath away!" Grace was shocked Nick had this romantic side. He had always been sweet and gentlemanly, but this was…over the top. They enjoyed the meal. It was five-star dining.

"Now that Paco's back…I'll be needing a place to live." Nick's eyes met hers.

"Stay at my place." Grace smiled. "You know I'd love to have you."

Nick reached his hand across the table and touched hers.

"Would you really love to have me?"

Her eyes locked with his.

"Yes. I would." Grace exhaled.

She watched as he reached for a tiny box on the table and slipped out a ring.

"Would you marry me, Grace? Be my wife? Wear this ring?"

Tears clouded her eyes, but she could see the ring was a unique, beautiful, a work of art.

"Where did you *get* this? How did you know my taste?"

He slipped the ring onto the ring finger of her left hand.

"The left hand is closest to the heart." He whispered. She felt the warmth of his hand around hers. Nick stood and moved toward Grace and she wrapped her arms around him.

"I'm sorry." She choked out the words. "I didn't expect this."

His hands cupped her face and his eyes sparked with passion. "I love you, Grace."

"Yes!" Grace whispered through tears. "My answer is yes, yes, yes."

~ THE END ~

Thank you for reading "Deep Blue Truth" ~ I greatly appreciate each and every reader. If you enjoyed the book, please leave a review for me on amazon.

Please check out my other books. I am a self-published independent author. That means I do everything from writing, to editing, publishing, designing the book covers to marketing. Your review means everything to me.

~ author, Ava Armstrong

Made in the USA
Columbia, SC
08 July 2018